Beasts
of the
Southern Wild
and
Other Stories

≠

DORIS BETTS

SCRIBNER PAPERBACK FICTION
Published by Simon & Schuster

To Max Steele

Contents

Contents

Beasts
of the
Southern Wild
and
Other Stories

The
Ugliest Pilgrim

I sit in the bus station, nipping chocolate peel off a Mounds candy bar with my teeth, then pasting the coconut filling to the roof of my mouth. The lump will dissolve there slowly and seep into me the way dew seeps into flowers.

I like to separate flavors that way. Always I lick the salt off cracker tops before taking my first bite.

Somebody sees me with my suitcase, paper sack, and a ticket in my lap. "You going someplace, Violet?"

Stupid. People in Spruce Pine are dumb and, since I look dumb, say dumb things to me. I turn up my face as if to count those dead flies piled under the light bulb. He walks away—a fat man, could be anybody. I stick out my tongue at his back; the candy oozes down. If I could stop swallowing, it would drip into my lung and I could breathe vanilla.

Whoever it was, he won't glance back. People in Spruce Pine don't like to look at me, full face.

A Greyhound bus pulls in, blows air; the driver stands by the door. He's black-headed, maybe part Cherokee, with heavy shoulders but a weak chest. He thinks well of himself—I can tell that. I open my notebook and copy his name off the metal plate so I can call him by it when he drives me home again. And next week, won't Mr. Wallace Weatherman be surprised to see how well I'm looking!

I choose the front seat behind Mr. Weatherman, settle my bag with the hat in it, then open the lined composition book again. Maybe it's half full of writing. Even the empty pages toward the back have one repeated entry, high, printed off Mama's torn catechism: GLORIFY GOD AND ENJOY HIM FOR-EVER.

I finish Mr. Weatherman off in my book while he's running his motor and getting us onto the highway. His nose is too broad, his dark eyes too skimpy—nothing in his face I want— but the hair is nice. I write that down, "Black hair?" I'd want it to curl, though, and be soft as a baby's.

Two others are on the bus, a nigger soldier and an old woman whose jaw sticks out like a shelf. There grow, on the backs of her hands, more veins than skin. One fat blue vessel, curling from wrist to knuckle, would be good; so on one page I draw a sample hand and let blood wind across it like a river. I write at the bottom: "Praise God, it is started. May 29, 1969," and turn to a new sheet. The paper's lumpy and I flip back to the thick envelope stuck there with adhesive tape. I can't lose that.

We're driving now at the best speed Mr. Weatherman can make on these winding roads. On my side there is nothing out the bus window but granite rock, jagged and wet in patches. The old lady and the nigger can see red rhododendron on the slope of Roan Mountain. I'd like to own a tight dress that flower color, and breasts to go under it. I write in my note-book, very small, the word "breasts," and turn quickly to another page. AND ENJOY HIM FOREVER.

The soldier bends as if to tie his shoes, but instead zips open a canvas bag and sticks both hands inside. When finally he sits back, one hand is clenched around something hard. He catches me watching. He yawns and scratches his ribs, but the right fist sets very lightly on his knee, and when I turn he drinks something out of its cup and throws his head quickly back like a bird or a chicken. You'd think I could smell it, big as my nose is.

Across the aisle the old lady says, "You going far?" She shows me a set of tan, artificial teeth.

"Oklahoma."

"I never been there. I hear the trees give out." She pauses so I can ask politely where she's headed. "I'm going to Nashville," she finally says. "The country-music capital of the world. My son lives there and works in the cellophane plant."

I draw in my notebook a box and two arrows. I crisscross the box.

"He's got three children not old enough to be in school yet."

I sit very still, adding new boxes, drawing baseballs in some, looking busy for fear she might bring out their pictures from her big straw pocketbook. The funny thing is she's looking past my head, though there's nothing out that window but rock wall sliding by. I mumble, "It's hot in here."

Angrily she says, "I had eight children myself."

My pencil flies to get the boxes stacked, eight-deep, in a pyramid. "Hope you have a nice visit."

"It's not a visit. I maybe will move." She is hypnotized by the stone and the furry moss in its cracks. Her eyes used to be green. Maybe, when young, she was red-haired and Irish. If she'll stop talking, I want to think about trying green eyes with that Cherokee hair. Her lids droop; she looks drowsy. "I am right tired of children," she says and lays her head back on the white rag they button on these seats.

Now that her eyes are covered, I can study that face—china white, and worn thin as tissue so light comes between her bones and shines through her whole head. I picture the light going around and around her skull, like water spinning in a jar. If I could wait to be eighty, even my face might grind down and look softer. But I'm ready, in case the Preacher mentions that. Did Elisha make Naaman bear into old age his leprosy? Didn't Jesus heal the withered hand, even on Sunday, without waiting for the work week to start? And put back the ear of Malchus with a touch? As soon as Job had learned enough, did his boils fall away?

Lord, I have learned enough.

The old lady sleeps while we roll downhill and up again; then we turn so my side of the bus looks over the valley and its thickety woods where, as a girl, I pulled armloads of galax, fern, laurel, and hemlock to have some spending money. I spent it for magazines full of women with permanent waves. Behind us, the nigger shuffles a deck of cards and deals to himself by fives. Draw poker—I could beat him. My papa showed me, long winter days and nights snowed in on the mountain. He said poker would teach me arithmetic. It taught me there are four ways to make a royal flush and, with two players, it's an even chance one of them holds a pair on the deal. And when you try to draw from a pair to four of a kind, discard the kicker; it helps your odds.

The soldier deals smoothly, using his left hand only with his thumb on top. Papa was good at that. He looks up and sees my whole face with its scar, but he keeps his eyes level as if he has seen worse things; and his left hand drops cards evenly and in rhythm. Like a turtle, laying eggs.

I close my eyes and the riffle of his deck rests me to the next main stop where I write in my notebook: "Praise God for Johnson City, Tennessee, and all the state to come. I am on my way."

At Kingsport, Mr. Weatherman calls rest stop and I go straight through the terminal to the ladies' toilet and look hard at my face in the mirror. I must remember to start the Preacher on the scar first of all—the only thing about me that's even on both sides.

Lord! I am so ugly!

Maybe the Preacher will claim he can't heal ugliness. And I'm going to spread my palms by my ears and show him—this is a crippled face! An infirmity! Would he do for a kidney or liver what he withholds from a face? The Preacher once stuttered, I read someplace, and God bothered with that. Why not me? When the Preacher labors to heal the sick in his Tulsa auditorium, he asks us at home to lay our fingers on the television screen and pray for God's healing. He puts forth his own ten fingers and we match them, pad to pad, on that glass. I have tried that, Lord, and the Power was too filtered and thinned down for me.

I touch my hand now to this cold mirror glass, and cover all but my pimpled chin, or wide nose, or a single red-brown eye. And nothing's too bad by itself. But when they're put together?

I've seen the Preacher wrap his hot, blessed hands on a club foot and cry out "HEAL!" in his funny way that sounds like the word "Hell" broken into two pieces. Will he not cry out, too, when he sees this poor, clubbed face? I will be to him as Goliath was to David, a need so giant it will drive God to action.

I comb out my pine-needle hair. I think I would like blond curls and Irish eyes, and I want my month so large it will never be done with kissing.

The old lady comes in the toilet and catches me pinching my bent face. She jerks back once, looks sad, then pets me with her twiggy hand. "Listen, honey," she says, "I had looks once. It don't amount to much."

I push right past. Good people have nearly turned me against you, Lord. They open their mouths for the milk of human kindness and boiling oil spews out.

So I'm half running through the terminal and into the café, and I take the first stool and call down the counter, "Tuna-fish sandwich," quick. Living in the mountains, I eat fish every chance I get and wonder what the sea is like. Then I see I've sat down by the nigger soldier. I do not want to meet his gaze, since he's a wonder to me, too. We don't have many black men in the mountains. Mostly they live east in Carolina, on the flatland, and pick cotton and tobacco instead of apples. They seem to me like foreigners. He's absently shuffling cards the way some men twiddle thumbs. On the stool beyond him is a paratrooper, white, and they're talking about what a bitch the army is. Being sent to the same camp has made them friends already.

I roll a dill-pickle slice through my mouth—a wheel, a bitter wheel. Then I start on the sandwich and it's chicken by mistake when I've got chickens all over my backyard.

"Don't bother with the beer," says the black one. "I've got better on the bus." They come to some agreement and deal out cards on the counter.

It's just too much for me. I lean over behind the nigger's back and say to the paratrooper, "I wouldn't play with him."

Neither one moves. "He's a mechanic." They look at each other, not at me. "It's a way to cheat on the deal."

The paratrooper sways backward on his stool and stares around out of eyes so blue that I want them, right away, and maybe his pale blond hair. I swallow a crusty half-chewed bite. "One-handed grip; the mechanic's grip. It's the middle finger. He can second-deal and bottom-deal. He can buckle the top card with his thumb and peep."

"I be damn," says the paratrooper.

The nigger spins around and bares his teeth at me, but it's half a grin. "Lady, you want to play?"

I slide my dishes back. "I get mad if I'm cheated."

"And mean when you're mad." He laughs a laugh so deep it makes me retaste that bittersweet chocolate off the candy bar. He offers the deck to cut, so I pull out the center and restack it three ways. A little air blows through his upper teeth. "I'm Grady Fliggins and they call me Flick."

The paratrooper reaches a hand down the counter to shake mine. "Monty Harrill. From near to Raleigh."

"And I'm Violet Karl. Spruce Pine. I'd rather play five-card stud."

By the time the bus rolls on, we've moved to its wider backseat playing serious cards with a fifty-cent ante. My money's sparse, but I'm good and the deck is clean. The old lady settles into my front seat, stiffer than plaster. Sometimes she throws back a hurt look.

Monty, the paratrooper, plays soft. But Flick's so good he doesn't even need to cheat, though I watch him close. He drops out quick when his cards are bad; he makes me bid high to see what he's got; and the few times he bluffs, I'm fooled. He's no talker. Monty, on the other hand, says often, "Whose play is it?" till I know that's his clue phrase for a pair. He lifts his cards close to his nose and gets quiet when planning to bluff. And he'd rather use wild cards but we won't. Ah, but he's pretty, though!

After we've swapped a little money, mostly the paratrooper's, Flick pours us a drink in some cups he stole in Kingsport and asks, "Where'd you learn to play?"

I tell him about growing up on a mountain, high, with Mama dead, and shuffling cards by a kerosene lamp with my papa. When I passed fifteen, we'd drink together, too. Applejack or a beer he made from potato peel.

"And where you headed now?" Monty's windburned in a funny pattern, with pale goggle circles that start high on his cheeks. Maybe it's something paratroopers wear.

"It's a pilgrimage." They lean back with their drinks. "I'm going to see this preacher in Tulsa, the one that heals, and I'm coming home pretty. Isn't that healing?" Their still faces make me nervous. "I'll even trade if he says. . . . I'll take somebody else's weak eyes or deaf ears. I could stand limping a little."

The nigger shakes his black head, snickering.

"I tried to get to Charlotte when he was down there with his eight-pole canvas cathedral tent that seats nearly fifteen thousand people, but I didn't have money then. Now what's so funny?" I think for a minute I am going to have to take out my notebook, and unglue the envelope and read them all the Scripture I have looked up on why I should be healed. Monty looks sad for me, though, and that's worse. "Let the Lord twist loose my foot or give me a cough, so long as I'm healed of my looks while I'm still young enough—" I stop and tip up my plastic cup. Young enough for you, blue-eyed boy, and your brothers.

"Listen," says Flick in a high voice. "Let me go with you and be there for that swapping." He winks one speckled eye.

"I'll not take black skin, no offense." He's offended, though, and lurches across the moving bus and falls into a far seat. "Well, you as much as said you'd swap it off!" I call. "What's wrong if I don't want it any more than you?"

Monty slides closer. "You're not much to look at," he grants, sweeping me up and down till I nearly glow blue from his eyes. Shaking his head, "And what now? Thirty?"

"Twenty-eight. His drink and his cards, and I hurt Flick's feelings. I didn't mean that." I'm scared, too. Maybe, unlike Job, I haven't learned enough. Who ought to be expert in hurt feelings? Me, that's who.

"And you live by yourself?"

I start to say "No, there's men falling all over each other going in and out my door." He sees my face, don't he? It makes me call, "Flick? I'm sorry." Not one movement. "Yes. By myself." Five years now, since Papa had heart failure and fell off the high back porch and rolled downhill in the gravel till the hobblebushes stopped him. I found him past sunset, cut from the rocks but not much blood showing. And what there was, dark, and already jellied.

Monty looks at me carefully before making up his mind to say, "That preacher's a fake. You ever see a doctor agree to what he's done?"

"Might be." I'm smiling. I tongue out the last liquor in my cup. I've thought of all that, but it may be what I believe is stronger than him faking. That he'll be electrified by my trust, the way a magnet can get charged against its will. He might be a lunatic or a dope fiend, and it still not matter.

Monty says, "Flick, you plan to give us another drink?"

"No." He acts like he's going to sleep.

"I just wouldn't count on that preacher too much." Monty cleans his nails with a matchbook corner and sometimes gives me an uneasy look. "Things are mean and ugly in this world —I mean *act* ugly, do ugly, be ugly."

He's wrong. When I leave my house, I can walk for miles and everything's beautiful. Even the rattlesnakes have grace. I don't mind his worried looks, since I'm writing in my notebook how we met and my winnings—a good sign, to earn money on a trip. I like the way army barbers trim his hair. I wish I could touch it.

"Took one furlough in your mountains. Pretty country. Maybe hard to live in? Makes you feel little." He looks toward Flick and says softer, "Makes you feel like the night sky does. So many stars."

"Some of them big as daisies." It's easy to live in, though. Some mornings a deer and I scare up each other in the brush, and his heart stops, and mine stops. Everything stops till he plunges away. The next pulsebeat nearly knocks you down. "Monty, doesn't your hair get lighter in the summers? That might be a good color hair to ask for in Tulsa. Then I could turn colors like the leaves. Spell your last name for me."

He does, and says I sure am funny. Then he spells Grady Fliggins and I write that, too. He's curious about my book, so I flip through and offer to read him parts. Even with his eyes shut, Flick is listening. I read them about my papa's face, a chunky block face, not much different from the Preacher's square one. After Papa died, I wrote that to slow down how fast I was forgetting him. I tell Monty parts of my lists: that you can get yellow dye out of gopherwood and Noah built his ark from that, and maybe it stained the water. That a cow eating snakeroot might give poison milk. I pass him a pressed maypop flower I'm carrying to Tulsa, because the crown of thorns and the crucifixion nails grow in its center, and each piece of the bloom stands for one of the apostles.

"It's a mollypop vine," says Flick out of one corner of his mouth. "And it makes a green ball that pops when you step on it." He stretches. "Deal you some blackjack?"

For no reason, Monty says, "We oughtn't to let her go."

We play blackjack till supper stop and I write in my book, "Praise God for Knoxville and two new friends." I've not had many friends. At school in the valley, I sat in the back rows, reading, a hand spread on my face. I was smart, too; but if you let that show, you had to stand for the class and present different things.

When the driver cuts out the lights, the soldiers give me a whole seat, and a duffelbag for a pillow. I hear them whispering, first about women, then about me; but after a while I don't hear that anymore.

By the time we hit Nashville, the old lady makes the bus wait while she begs me to stop with her. "Harvey won't mind. He's a good boy." She will not even look at Monty and Flick. "You can wash and change clothes and catch a new bus tomorrow."

"I'm in a hurry. Thank you." I have picked a lot of galax to pay for this trip.

"A girl alone. A girl that maybe feels she's got to prove something?" The skin on her neck shivers. "Some people might take advantage."

Maybe when I ride home under my new face, that will be some risk. I shake my head, and as she gets off she whispers something to Mr. Weatherman about looking after me. It's wasted, though, because a new driver takes his place and he looks nearly as bad as I do—oily-faced and toad-shaped, with eyeballs a dingy color and streaked with blood. He's the flatlands driver, I guess, because he leans back and drops one warty hand on the wheel and we go so fast and steady you can hardly tell it.

Since Flick is the tops in cards and we're tired of that, it's Monty's turn to brag on his motorcycle. He talks all across Tennessee till I think I could ride one by hearsay alone, that my wrist knows by itself how far to roll the throttle in. It's a Norton and he rides it in Scrambles and Enduro events, in his leathers, with spare parts and tools glued all over him with black electrician's tape.

"So this bastard tells me, 'Zip up your jacket because when I run over you I want some traction.'"

Flick is playing solitaire. "You couldn't get me on one of them killing things."

"One day I'm coming through Spruce Pine, flat out, throw Violet up behind me! We're going to lean all the way through them mountains. Sliding the right foot and then sliding the left." Monty lays his head back on the seat beside me, rolls it, watches. "How you like that? Take you through creeks and ditches like you was on a skateboard. You can just holler and hang on."

Lots of women have, I bet.

"The Norton's got the best front forks of anybody. It'll nearly roll up a tree trunk and ride down the other side." He demonstrates on the seat back. I keep writing. These are new things, two-stroke and four-stroke, picking your line on a curve, Milwaukee iron. It will all come back to me in the winters, when I reread these pages.

Flick says he rode on a Harley once. "Turned over and got drug. No more."

They argue about what he should have done instead of

turning over. Finally Monty drifts off to sleep, his head leaning at me slowly, so I look down on his crisp, light hair. I pat it
as easy as a cat would, and it tickles my palm. I'd almost ask
them in Tulsa to make me a man if I could have hair like his,
and a beard, and feel so different in so many places.

He slides closer in his sleep. One eyebrow wrinkles against
my shoulder. Looking our way, Flick smokes a cigarette, then
reads some magazine he keeps rolled in his belt. Monty
makes a deep noise against my arm as if, while he slept, his
throat had cleared itself. I shift and his whole head is on my
shoulder now. Its weight makes me breathe shallow.

I rest my eyes. If I should turn, his hair would barely touch
my cheek, the scarred one, like a shoebrush. I do turn and it
does. For miles he sleeps that way and I almost sleep. Once,
when we take a long curve, he rolls against me, and one of his
hands drifts up and then drops in my lap. Just there, where
the creases are.

I would not want God's Power to turn me, after all, into a
man. His breath is so warm. Everywhere, my skin is singing.
Praise God for that.

When I get my first look at the Mississippi River, the pencil
goes straight into my pocketbook. How much praise would
that take?

"Is the sea like this?"

"Not except they're both water," Flick says. He's not mad
anymore. "Tell you what, Vi-oh-LETTE. When Monty picks
you up on his cycle" ("sickle," he calls it), "you ride down to
the beaches—Cherry Grove, O.D., around there. Where they
work the big nets in the fall and drag them up on the sand
with trucks at each end, and men to their necks in the surf."

"You do that?"

"I know people that do. And afterward they strip and dress by this big fire on the beach."

And they make chowder while this cold wind is blowing! I know that much, without asking. In a big black pot that sits on that whipping fire. I think they might let me sit with them and stir the pot. It's funny how much, right now, I feel like praising all the good things I've never seen, in places I haven't been.

Everybody has to get off the bus and change in Memphis, and most of them wait a long time. I've taken the long way, coming here; but some of Mama's cousins live in Memphis and might rest me overnight. Monty says they plan to stay the night, too, and break the long trip.

"They know you're coming, Violet?" It's Flick says my name that way, in pieces, carefully: Vi-oh-LETTE. Monty is lazier: Viii-lut. They make me feel like more than one.

"I've never even met these cousins. But soon as I call up and tell them who I am and that I'm here . . ."

"We'll stay some hotel tonight and then ride on. Why don't you come with us?" Monty is carrying my scuffed bag. Flick swings the paper sack. "You know us better than them."

"Kin people," grunts Flick, "can be a bad surprise."

Monty is nodding his head. "Only cousin I had got drunk and drove this tractor over his baby brother. Did it on purpose, too." I see by his face that Monty has made this up, for my sake.

"Your cousins might not even live here anymore. I bet it's been years since you heard from a one."

"We're picking a cheap hotel, in case that's a worry."

I never thought they might have moved. "How cheap?"

When Flick says "Under five," I nod; and my things go right up on their shoulders as I follow them into a Memphis cab. The driver takes for granted I'm Monty's afflicted sister and names a hotel right off. He treats me with pity and good manners.

And the hotel he chooses is cheap, all right, where ratty salesmen with bad territories spend half the night drinking in their rooms. Plastic palm bushes and a worn rug the color of wet cigars. I get Room 210 and they're down the hall in the teens. They stand in my doorway and watch me drop both shoes and walk the bed in bare feet. When Monty opens my window, we can hear some kitchen underneath—a fan, clattering noise, a man's crackly voice singing about the California earthquake.

It scares me, suddenly, to know I can't remember how home sounds. Not one bird call, nor the water over rocks. There's so much you can't save by writing down.

"Smell that grease," says Flick, and shakes his head till his lips flutter. "I'm finding an ice machine. You, Vi-oh-LETTE, come on down in a while."

Monty's got a grin I'll remember if I never write a word. He waves. "Flick and me going to get drunker than my old cousin and put wild things in your book. Going to draw dirty pictures. You come on down and get drunk enough to laugh."

But after a shower, damp in my clean slip, even this bed like a roll of fence wire feels good, and I fall asleep wondering if that rushing noise is a river wind, and how long I can keep it in my mind.

Monty and Flick edge into my dream. Just their voices first, from way downhill. Somewhere in a Shonny Haw thicket. "Just different," Monty is saying. "That's all. Different. Don't make some big thing out of it." He doesn't sound happy. "Nobody else," he says.

Is that Flick singing? No, because the song goes on while

his voice says, "Just so . . ." and then some words I don't catch. "It don't hurt"? Or maybe, "You don't hurt"? I hear them climbing my tangled hill, breaking sticks and knocking the little stones loose. I'm trying to call to them which way the path is, but I can't make noise because the Preacher took my voice and put it in a black bag and carried it to a sick little boy in Iowa.

They find the path, anyway. And now they can see my house and me standing little by the steps. I know how it looks from where they are: the wood rained on till the siding's almost silver; and behind the house a wet-weather waterfall that's cut a stream bed downhill and grown pin cherry and bee balm on both sides. The high rock walls by the waterfall are mossy and slick, but I've scraped one place and hammered a mean-looking gray head that leans out of the hillside and stares down the path at whoever comes. I've been here so long by myself that I talk to it sometimes. Right now I'd say, "Look yonder. We've got company at last!" if my voice wasn't gone.

"You can't go by looks," Flick is saying as they climb. He ought to know. Ahead of them, warblers separate and fly out on two sides. Everything moves out of their path if I could just see it—tree frogs and mosquitoes. Maybe the worms drop deeper just before a footstep falls.

"Without the clothes, it's not a hell of a lot improved," says Monty, and I know suddenly they are inside the house with me, inside my very room, and my room today's in Memphis. "There's one thing, though," Monty says, standing over my bed. "Good looks in a woman is almost like a wall. She can use it to shut you outside. You never know what she's like, that's all." He's wearing a T-shirt and his dog tags jingle. "Most of the time I don't even miss knowing that."

And Flick says, disgusted, "I knew that much in grammar school. You sure are slow. It's not the face you screw." If I opened my eyes, I could see him now, behind Monty. He says, "After a while, you don't even notice faces. I always thought, in a crowd, my mother might not pick Daddy out."

"*My* mother could," says Monty. "He was always the one *started* the fight."

I stretch and open my eyes. It's a plain slip, cotton, that I sewed myself and makes me look too white and skinny as a sapling.

"She's waking up."

When I point, Monty hands me the blouse off the door-knob. Flick says they've carried me a soda pop, plus something to spruce it up. They sit stiffly on two hard chairs till I've buttoned on my skirt. I sip the drink, cold but peppery, and prop on the bed with the pillows. "I dreamed you both came where my house is, on the mountain, and it had rained so the waterfall was working. I felt real proud of that."

After two drinks we go down to the noisy restaurant with that smelly grease. And after that, to a picture show. Monty grins widely when the star comes on the screen. The spit on his teeth shines, even in the dark. Seeing what kind of woman he really likes, black-haired as a gypsy and with a juicy mouth, I change all my plans. My eyes, too, must turn up on the ends and when I bend down my breasts must fall forward and push at each other. When the star does that in the picture, the cow-boy rubs his mustache low in the front of her neck.

In the darkness, Monty takes my hand and holds it in his swelling lap. To me it seems funny that my hand, brown and crusty from hoeing and chopping, is harder than his. I guess you don't get calluses rolling a motorcycle throttle. He rubs his thumb up and down my middle finger. Oh, I would like to ride

27

fast behind him, spraddle-legged, with my arms wrapped on his belt, and I would lay my face between his sharp shoulder blades.

That night, when I've slept awhile, I hear something brushing the rug in the hall. I slip to my door. It's very dark. I press myself, face first, to the wood. There's breathing on the other side. I feel I get fatter, standing there, that even my own small breasts might now be made to touch. I round both shoulders to see. The movement jars the door and it trembles slightly in its frame.

From the far side, by the hinges, somebody whispers, "Vi-oh-LETTE?"

Now I stand very still. The wood feels cooler on my skin, or else I have grown very warm. Oh, I could love anybody! There is so much of me now, they could line up strangers in the hall and let me hold each one better than he had ever been held before!

Slowly I turn the knob, but Flick's breathing is gone. The corridor's empty. I leave the latch off.

Late in the night, when the noise from the kitchen is over, he comes into my room. I wake when he bumps on a chair, swears, then scrabbles at the footboard.

"Viii-lut?"

I slide up in bed. I'm not ready, not now, but he's here. I spread both arms wide. In the dark he can't tell.

He feels his way onto the bed and he touches my knee and it changes. Stops being just my old knee, under his fingers. I feel the joint heat up and bubble. I push the sheet down.

He comes onto me, whispering something. I reach up to claim him.

One time he stops. He's surprised, I guess, finding he isn't the first. How can I tell him how bad that was? How long ago? The night when the twelfth grade was over and one of them climbed with me all the way home? And he asked. And I thought, *I'm entitled.* Won him a five-dollar bet. Didn't do nothing for me.

But this time I sing out and Monty says, "Shh," in my ear. And he starts over, slow, and makes me whimper one other time. Then he turns sideways to sleep and I try my face there, laid in the nest on his damp back. I reach out my tongue. He is salty and good.

Now there are two things too big for my notebook but praise God! And for the Mississippi, too!

There is no good reason for me to ride with them all the way to Fort Smith, but since Tulsa is not expecting me, we change my ticket. Monty pays the extra. We ride through the fertile plains. The last of May becomes June and the Arkansas sun is blazing. I am stunned by this heat. At home, night means blankets and even on hot afternoons it may rain and start the waterfall. I lie against my seat for miles without a word.

"What's wrong?" Monty keeps asking; but, under the heat, I am happy. Sleepy with happiness, a lizard on a rock. At every stop Monty's off the bus, bringing me more than I can eat or drink, buying me magazines and gum. I tell him and Flick to play two-handed cards, but mostly Flick lectures him in a low voice about something.

I try to stop thinking of Memphis and think back to Tulsa. I went to the Spruce Pine library to look up Tulsa in their encyclopedia. I thought sure it would tell about the Preacher, and on what street he'd built his Hope and Glory Building for his soul crusades. Tulsa was listed in the *Americana*, Volume 27,

Trance to Venial Sin. I got so tickled with that I forgot to write down the rest.

Now, in the hot sun, clogged up with trances and venial sins, I dream under the drone of their voices. For some reason I remember that old lady back in Nashville, moved in with Harvey and his wife and their three children. I hope she's happy. I picture her on Harvey's back porch, baked in the sun like me, in a rocker. Snapping beans.

I've left my pencil in the hotel and must borrow one from Flick to write in my book. I put in, slowly, "This is the day which the Lord hath made." But, before Monty, what kind of days was He sending me? I cross out the line. I have this wish to praise, instead of Him, the littlest things. Honeybees, and the wet slugs under their rocks. A gnat in some farmer's eye.

I give up and hand Flick his pencil. He slides toward the aisle and whispers, "You wish you'd stayed in your mountains?"

I shake my head and a piece of my no-color hair falls into the sunlight. Maybe it even shines.

He spits on the pencil point and prints something inside a gum wrapper. "Here's my address. You keep it. Never can tell."

So I tear the paper in half and give him back mine. He reads it a long time before tucking it away, but he won't send a letter till I do—I can tell that. Through all this, Monty stares out the window. Arkansas rolls out ahead of us like a rug.

Monty has not asked for my address, nor how far uphill I live from Spruce Pine, though he could ride his motorcycle up to me, strong as its engine is. For a long time he has been sitting quietly, lighting one cigarette off another. This winter,

I've got to learn smoking. How to lift my hand up so every eye will follow it to my smooth cheek.

I put Flick's paper in my pocketbook and there, inside, on a round mirror, my face is waiting in ambush for me. I see the curved scar, neat as ever, swoop from the edge of one nostril in rainbow shape across my cheek, then down toward the ear. For the first time in years, pain boils across my face as it did that day. I close my eyes under that red drowning, and see again Papa's ax head rise off its locust handle and come float-ing through the air, sideways, like a gliding crow. And it drops down into my face almost daintily, the edge turned just enough to slash loose a flap of skin the way you might slice straight down on the curve of a melon. My papa is yelling, but I am under a red rain and it bears me down. I am lifted and run with through the woodyard and into the barn. Now I am slumped on his chest and the whipped horse is throwing us down the mountainside, and my head is wrapped in some-thing big as a wet quilt. The doctor groans when he winds it off and I faint while he lifts up my flesh like the flap of a pulpy envelope, and sews the white bone out of sight.

Dizzy from the movement of the bus, I snap shut my pocketbook.

Whenever I cry, the first drop quivers there, in the curving scar, and then runs crooked on that track to the ear. I cry straight-down on the other side.

I am glad this bus has a toilet. I go there to cool my eyes with wet paper, and spit up Monty's chocolate and cola.

When I come out, he's standing at the door with his fist up. "You all right, Viii-lut? You worried or something?"

I see he pities me. In my seat again, I plan the speech I will make at Fort Smith and the laugh I will give. "Honey, you're good," I'll say, laughing, "but the others were better." That ought to do it. I am quieter now than Monty is, practicing it in my mind.

It's dark when we hit Fort Smith. Everybody's face looks shadowed and different. Mine better. Monty's strange. We're saying good-byes very fast. I start my speech twice and he misses it twice.

Then he bends over me and offers his own practiced line that I see he's worked up all across Arkansas, "I plan to be right here, Violet, in this bus station. On Monday. All day. You get off your bus when it comes through. Hear me, Viii-lut? I'll watch for you?"

No. He won't watch. Nor I come. "My schedule won't take me this road going back. Bye, Flick. Lots of good luck to you both."

"Promise me. Like I'm promising."

"Good luck to you, Vi-oh-LETTE." Flick lets his hand fall on my head and it feels as good as anybody's hand.

Monty shoves money at me and I shove it back. "Promise," he says, his voice furious. He tries to kiss me in the hair and I jerk so hard my nose cracks his chin. We stare, blurry-eyed and hurting. He follows Flick down the aisle, calls back, "I'm coming here Monday. See you then, hear? And you get off this bus!"

"No! I won't!"

He yells it twice more. People are staring. He's out of the bus pounding on the steel wall by my seat. I'm not going to look. The seats fill up with strangers and we ride away, nobody talking to anyone else. My nose where I hit it is going to swell —the Preacher will have to throw that in for free. I look back, but he's gone.

The lights in the bus go out again. Outside they bloom thick by the streets, then thinner, then mostly gone as we pass into the countryside. Even in the dark, I can see Oklahoma's mountains are uglier than mine. Knobs and hills, mostly. The bus drives into rain which covers up everything. At home I like that washing sound. We go deeper into the downpour. Perhaps we are under the Arkansas River, after all. It seems I can feel its great weight move over me.

Before daylight, the rain tapers off and here the ground looks dry, even barren. Cattle graze across long fields. In the wind, wheat fields shiver. I can't eat anything all the way to Tulsa. It makes me homesick to see the land grow brighter and flatter and balder. That old lady was right—the trees do give out—and oil towers grow in their place. The glare's in my eyes. I write in my notebook, "Praise God for Tulsa; I am nearly there," but it takes a long time to get the words down.

One day my papa told me how time got slow for him when Mama died. How one week he waded through the creek and it was water, and the next week cold molasses. How he'd lay awake a year between sundown and sunup, and in the morning I'd be a day older and he'd be three hundred and sixty-five.

It works the other way, too. In no time at all, we're into Tulsa without me knowing what we've passed. So many tall buildings. Everybody's running. They rush into taxis before I can get one to wait for me long enough to ask the driver questions. But still I'm speeded to a hotel, and the elevator yanks me to a room quicker than Elijah rode to Heaven. The room's not bad. A Gideon Bible. Inside are lots of dirty words somebody wrote. He must have been feeling bad.

I bathe and dress, trembling from my own speed, and pin on the hat which has traveled all the way from Spruce Pine for this. I feel tired. I go out into the loud streets full of fast cars. Hot metal everywhere. A taxi roars me across town to the Preacher's church.

It looks like a big insurance office, though I can tell where the chapel is by colored glass in the pointed windows. Carved in an arch over the door are the words "HOPE OF GLORY BUILD-ING." Right away, something in me sinks. All this time I've been hearing it on TV as the Hope *and* Glory Building. You wouldn't think one word could make that much difference.

Inside the door, there's a list of offices and room numbers. I don't see the Preacher's name. Clerks send me down long, tiled halls, past empty air-conditioned offices. One tells me to go up two flights and ask the fat woman, and the fat woman sends me down again. I'm carrying my notebook in a dry hand, feeling as brittle as the maypop flower.

At last I wait an hour to see some assistant—very close to the Preacher, I'm told. His waiting room is chilly, the leatherette chairs worn down to the mesh. I try to remember how much TB and cancer have passed through this very room and been jerked out of people the way Jesus tore out a demon and flung him into a herd of swine. I wonder what he felt like to the swine.

After a long time, the young man calls me into his plain office—wood desk, wood chairs. Shelves of booklets and col-ored folders. On one wall, a colored picture of Jesus with that fairy ring of light around His head. Across from that, one of His praying hands—rougher than Monty's, smoother than mine.

The young man wears glasses with no rims. In this glare, I am reflected on each lens, Vi-oh-LETTE and Viii-lut. On his desk is a box of postcards of the Hope and Glory Building. *Of* Glory. *Of* Glory.

I am afraid.

I feel behind me for the chair.

The man explains that he is presently in charge. The Preacher's speaking in Tallahassee, his show taped weeks ahead. I never thought of it as a show before. He waits.

I reach inside my notebook where, taped shut, is the thick envelope with everything written down. I knew I could never explain things right. When have I ever been able to tell what I really felt? But it's all in there—my name, my need. The words from the Bible which must argue for me. I did not sit there nights since Papa died, counting my money and studying God's Book, for nothing. Playing solitaire, then going back to search the next page and the next. Stepping outside to rest my eyes on His limitless sky, then back to the Book and the paper, building my case.

He starts to read, turns up his glitter-glass to me once to check how I look, then reads again. His chair must be hard, for he squirms in it, crosses his legs. When he has read every page, he lays the stack down, slowly takes off his glasses, folds them shining into a case. He leaves it open on his desk. Mica shines like that, in the rocks.

Then he looks at me, fully. Oh. He is plain. Almost homely. I nearly expected it. Maybe Samuel was born ugly, so who else would take him but God?

"My child," the man begins, though I'm older than he is, "I understand how you feel. And we will most certainly pray for your spirit. . . ."

I shut my eyes against those two flashing faces on his spectacles. "Never mind my spirit." I see he doesn't really understand. I see he will live a long life, and not marry.

"Our Heavenly Father has purpose in all things."

Stubbornly, "Ask Him to set it aside."

"We must all trust His will."

After all these years, isn't it God's turn to trust mine? Could He not risk a little beauty on me? Just when I'm ready to ask, the sober assistant recites, " 'Favor is deceitful and beauty is vain.' That's in Proverbs."

And I cry, " 'The crooked shall be made straight!' Isaiah said that!" He draws back, as if I had brought the Gideon Bible and struck him with its most disfigured pages. "Jesus healed an impediment in speech. See my impediment! Mud on a blind man's eyes was all He needed! Don't you remember?" But he's read all that. Everything I know on my side lies, written out, under his sweaty hand. Lord, don't let me whine. But I whine, "He healed the ten lepers and only one thanked. Well, I'll thank. I promise. All my life."

He clears his long knotty throat and drones like a bee, " 'By the sadness of the countenance the heart is made better.' Ecclesiastes. Seven. Three."

Oh, that's not fair! I skipped those parts, looking for verses that suited me! And it's wrong, besides.

I get up to leave and he asks will I kneel with him? "Let us pray together for that inner beauty."

No, I will not. I go down that hollow hall and past the echoing rooms. Without his help I find the great auditorium, lit through colored glass, with its cross of white plastic and a pinker Jesus molded onto it. I go straight to the pulpit where the Preacher stands. There is nobody else to plead. I ask Jesus not to listen to everything He hears, but to me only.

Then I tell Him how it feels to be ugly, with nothing to look back at you but a deer or an owl. I read Him my paper, out loud, full of His own words.

"I have been praising you, Lord, but it gets harder every year." Maybe that sounds too strong. I try to ease up my tone before the Amens. Then the chapel is very quiet. For one minute I hear the whir of many wings, but it's only a fan inside an air vent.

I go into the streets of Tulsa, where even the shade from a building is hot. And as I walk to the hotel I'm repeating, over and over, "Praise God for Tulsa in spite of everything."

Maybe I say this aloud, since people are staring. But maybe that's only because they've never seen a girl cry crooked in their streets before.

Monday morning. I have not looked at my face since the pulpit prayer. Who can predict how He might act—with a lightning bolt? Or a melting so slow and tender it could not even be felt?

Now, on the bus, I can touch in my pocketbook the cold mirror glass. Though I cover its surface with prints, I never look down. We ride through the dust and I'm nervous. My pencil is flying: "Be ye therefore perfect as your Heavenly Father is perfect. Praise God for Oklahoma. For Wagoner and Sapulpa and Broken Arrow and every other name on these signs by the road."

Was that the wrong thing to tell Him? My threat that even praise can be withheld? Maybe He's angry. "Praise God for oil towers whether I like them or not." When we pass churches, I copy their names. Praise them all. I want to write, "Bless," but that's *His* job.

We cross the cool Arkansas River. As its damp rises into the bus and touches my face, something wavers there, in the very bottom of each pore; and I clap my rough hands to each cheek. Maybe He's started? How much can He do between here and Fort Smith? If He will?

For I know what will happen. Monty won't come. And I won't stop. That's an end to it.

No, Monty is there. Waiting right now. And I'll go into the bus station on tiptoe and stand behind him. He'll turn, with his blue eyes like lamps. *And he won't know me!* If I'm changed. So I will explain myself to him: how this gypsy hair and this juicy mouth is still Violet Karl. He'll say, "Won't old Flick be surprised?" He'll say, "Where is that place you live? Can I come there?"

But if, while I wait and he turns, he should know me by my old face . . . If he should say my name or show by recognition that my name's rising up now in his eyes like something through water . . . I'll be running by then. To the bus. Straight out that door to the Tennessee bus, saying, "Driver, don't let that man on!" It's a very short stop. We'll be pulling out quick. I don't think he'll follow, anyhow.

I don't even think he will come.

One hundred and thirty-one miles to Fort Smith. I wish I could eat.

I try to think up things to look forward to at home. Maybe the sourwoods are blooming early, and the bees have been laying-by my honey. If it's rained enough, my corn might be in tassel. Wouldn't it be something if God took His own sweet time, and I lived on that slope for years and years, getting prettier all the time? And nobody to know?

It takes nearly years and years to get to Fort Smith. My papa knew things about time. I comb out my hair, not looking once to see what color sheddings are caught in the teeth. There's no need feeling my cheek, since my finger expects that scar. I can feel it on me almost anywhere, by memory. I straighten my skirt and lick my lips till the spit runs out.

And they're waiting. Monty at one door of the terminal and Flick at another.

"Ten minutes," the driver says when the bus is parked, but I wait in my seat till Flick gets restless and walks to the cigarette machine. Then I slip through his entrance door and inside the station. Mirrors shine everywhere. On the vending machines and the weight machines and a full-length one by the phone booth. It's all I can do not to look. I pass the ticket window and there's Monty's back at the other door. My face remembers the shape of it. Seeing him there, how he's made, and the parts of him fitted, makes me forget how I look. And before I can stop, I call out his name.

Right away, turning, he yells to me "*Viii*-lut!"

So I know. I can look, then, in the wide mirror over a jukebox. Tired as I am and unfed, I look worse than I did when I started from home.

He's laughing and talking. "I been waiting here since daylight scared you wouldn't . . ." but by then I've run past the ugly girl in the glass and I race for the bus, for the road, for the mountain.

Behind me, he calls loudly, "Flick!"

I see that one step in my path like a floating dark blade, but I'm faster this time. I twist by him, into the flaming sun and the parking lot. How my breath hurts!

Monty's between me and my bus, but there's time. I circle the cabstand, running hard over the asphalt field, with a pain ticking in my side. He calls me. I plunge through the crowd like a deer through fetterbush. But he's running as hard as he can and he's faster than me. And, oh!

Praise God!

He's catching me!

Hitchhiker

She woke that morning angry about something—perhaps a dream?—she could not recall. Her tongue was dusty. She drank two glasses of water with the aspirin. Belching the bitter gas of coffee, she threw her breakfast dishes into the sink and promised herself *no more parties.*

No more losing sleep to hear stupid people talk for a hundred years about things that did not matter. To her, to them, to anybody. No more diluting bad parties with gin and bourbon; after midnight she'd have swallowed gasoline had someone poured it in her glass. Now her whole body was nasty with alcohol. Black slime and swamp gas.

She wrapped herself in dark clothes, stepped into flat shoes, and carried her books to the car, which smelled of rubber and the skin of dead animals. The steering wheel was dimpled underneath to fit her grip. Yet there was no place she wanted to go, least of all to the next city to work. She opened the car door and spat onto the greasy cement a wad of the snot which had leaked into her mouth. Then she pulled out of the garage and hooked her car onto a row of others on the highway, like a link on a chain.

The party. Max had explained Wall Street to her, especially "futures," where men bought abstract bacon they did not want delivered, which—indeed—did not exist; and then sold it again. A lawyer discussed the importance of making demands no court would grant so cases could be settled nearer his real demands. All evening she had crossed and recrossed Max's living room like a languid billiard ball, thumping in one group against Catholicism and the Pill, in another the need of the Vietnamese peace talks to have square or round tables, and in a third an argument about the Apollo space flight around the moon. Someone insisted the astronauts, once out of sight, wheeled patiently in space and sent back false reports as a boost to the nation's self-esteem. An advertising man, it was claimed, had promoted the whole idea of faking three wise men aloft at Christmas. "Oh, for Christ's sake!" she'd said—to a bearded student who turned out to be in seminary.

The string of cars reached the four-lane interstate route, and she pulled out to pass a long metal line. The wind rushed and subsided in a series of gasps as she went by, swung uphill free of them, and turned left onto the narrow road which would take her thirty miles to the Research Company, Inc., where all day she would sit in a frosted-glass box and type polysyllables.

She reached for the plastic jar of aspirins she kept in a niche by the windshield and chewed three. Lyons Motor Court, with its neon lion. The Bar-B-Q Barn. Then she was into wooded countryside on a looping, slow highway the trucks and salesmen avoided, and she could slow down and watch the pines come toward her, split, and pass on both sides. The sun through the window glass melted her flat on the seat, and the regular slap of her tires on the asphalt lines made her drowsy. A young woman tried to wave down a ride, but she did not stop.

Ahead of her, the solid concrete bridge across the first river split at the last minute into two walls, and swept by. There was a woman atop the hill with her thumb out; she wore a red dress. She appeared, tiny in the rearview mirror, like a blood spot in an egg.

She turned on the car radio. The *Pueblo* had been released by North Korea. American negotiators explained it was necessary to confess the *Pueblo* was a spy ship in order to free the crewmen. The apologetic statement was read over the air, along with its repudiation. As she turned off the news, she saw another woman hitchhiker, also in red, but older than the others. She did not want to get to work, and drove more slowly. The lumps on the steering wheel were sculpted in the wrong places and would not fit between her fingers. She clasped and unclasped her damp palms.

Her name was Duffy. Rose Marie Duffy, although only the last name appeared on the plastic breastpin the gate guard handed her every morning at the plant. She dreaded the pin, the baked parking lot. She dreaded walking down the halls, passing executives who would say, "Good morning, Miss . . ." and squint at her chest before they added, "Duffy." Especially she dreaded all that today, for Friday had been a busy day, and she had bent a key on her typewriter. Friday she had been typing a report in the usual way and had glanced down at the center row of lettered tabs on which her fingers rested as lightly as moths. She could have typed them blind, in the dark, after a hundred years of being away from typewriters. ASDFG might as well have been tattooed across her left knuckles. HJKL; on the right. And suddenly, like a message springing up from heretofore invisible ink, she had read on her own skin, "Ass, Duffy. Go Home, Jekyll." She stared at the—anagram, was it? Cryptogram? Hallucination? Then she had to type the whole page over after jamming the keys. After that the bottom row of keys set up a buzzing hum in her ears. "ZXCVBNM, ZXCVBNM," they said, like beetles.

She stared at the face of the typewriter, and then read in the first two rows:

Queer tie, you hope
As daffy go highjinkle

No, that second line was wrong. "As differ gherkin jackels." She started over with the top row of letters. "Kew wert? Why, you, I hope!" Despairing, Duffy felt if she had only known Latin she could have made all twenty-six letters arrange themselves into three lines, like a litany, and it would have been comforting to whisper to herself.

But that was on Friday, and by now Duffy would not have cared if one swipe to clean the typewriter keys had brought forth steam and a genie. She would not have been very much surprised, either.

She drove through Pitchfield, a village with three stores and a bankrupt movie house which had been for sale two years or more. Beyond the town, Negroes lived on each side of the highway in paired rows of black, weathered houses. There were fifty children living on each side of the road, and every time she passed they were all in their front yards, yelling across her car to their counterparts on the other side. Their voices made her feel rained upon. She passed now their gray church, parked even on weekdays with used cars. Someone was catching a nap behind the church, wrapped in a red cloth and curled on a mat of pine needles.

Duffy drove upward, the land pulling, to the hilltop from

which she would see the second river. Every morning she looked forward to the view, as the river wound out of a pasture and forest, churned by a little island it had spit up, and fell down a low man-made waterfall just beyond the bridge. In the fall, the far hillside ran red and gold, and in spring the first leaves made it misty with color that wasn't green yet but soon would be. Now it was green, dulled by the August drought. Duffy rolled up her windows, for the river was the urinary tract for five paper mills and its waters stank.

Then—had she planned it?—she crested the hill, swept down, and at the last minute jerked the wheel to the right and drove straight down the rocky bank into the river.

The current was sluggish and she had no difficulty turning into it, the brown water halfway up her windows, and heading downstream. It was a great relief to drive at the river's speed, so that she went between the shrouded banks instead of seeing them pour headlong toward her face, and separate reluctantly to let her car pass through. She leaned back and read the dashboard of her car: "Temp," "Fan," and "Def," it said, "Oil," "Gen," and "Speed." The words matched the tune of the Navy Hymn, "Eternal Father, Strong to Save," and she liked them much better and sang as she sailed. The doors were leaking, but she had lived so long with leakage that the rivulets seemed an artistic pattern, streaking the car's lining with an abstract design. The motor gurgled, drank deep, and ended. Duffy laid her head against the seat, watching shadows fall on the water ahead of the car and pour through the windshield, cool on her face. She closed her eyes and could still see them, through her eyelids, like clouds.

When she fell asleep, she dreamed she was working in her cubicle at the Research Company. She had misspelled some long and rippling word. When she erased it, a space appeared in the paper like a small transparent window. Curiously, she scrubbed the eraser on another word and it turned to air. In her dream she laughed, erasing the entire page, paper and all, until there was nothing left but some rubber shavings and, tattooed in midair, a translucent watermark.

When she awoke, the car had beached itself on a sandbar. Her door was jammed and she felt like a biscuit in an oven. Duffy rolled down the window and beat on the hot metal side. She could see nothing but the brown river, forest on both sides. She took off everything but her underwear and wriggled painfully out the window, feet first. She dropped ankle-deep in the yellow sand.

The sandbar was round, not much larger than the car itself. It rose above the water like a bald head with a few tufts of grass around the rim. Duffy circled it, but there was nothing to see except the thick woods. She waded out on the narrow side, but the water rose swiftly and she scrambled back ashore. She tried the horn, but it only sighed. Then she stood by the driver's seat, hands on wet hips, and yelled for help. Because she felt there was something orderly about it, she screamed from the trunk of the car, the other side, the grille, and sent her need radiating in four directions. She lay in the sun and waited for help to come.

At sundown, a fisherman in a motorboat, headed upstream, spotted Duffy's car and picked her up. "I thought it was some TV commercial at first," he said with a laugh, turning the way he had come. "The car set down by a helicopter or something. And you in your underwear—well, what else could it be?" He laughed for miles downstream while Duffy huddled low in the boat, hugging herself and shivering. She wondered where the mosquitoes were. "It's a long ride," he said. "No houses here. People have left the river. I fish it every night, and there wasn't no car stuck out there yesterday. I tell you, I looked everyplace for the cameras."

The water stank so bad Duffy asked him how a fish could live in it, and he said none could; that was his job, rescue work. Getting them into the air. He ran his motor at speed and they flew through the water so fast that Duffy was dizzy. "My daddy used to fish," she said, but he couldn't hear her for the roar.

She was cold in the whipping wind. They seemed to be rushing from day into dark, and the river grew narrow as the trees and their long shadows leaned thicker from the banks. "How far is it? I'm cold." He stared straight ahead. If they struck a rock at this speed, she thought, they'd both be thrown, flapping, like water birds. Like terrified water birds. That was a nice word, "terrified." She said it under her breath, because it was what she should have been when she drove off the bridge. Perhaps she could be it yet, by will.

"I hope we get there in time," said the fisherman. She did not know in time for what. They roared downstream a long way before the first lights were seen, a window there, a whole building ablaze. He cut their speed. In the dark she could see nothing but the isolated squares of light, some large, some no bigger than cat eyes.

He said, "You cold?" He handed her something, a garment, sleazy to the touch. Old taffeta, perhaps, or faille. It would not wrap her and she fumbled for its shape. A dress. She shook it out to find the neck and sleeves, then pulled it over her head.

"Now," he said, throwing one arm toward the lights which lay at random on either side. The water was a looping ribbon now, wide enough for two boats if they passed carefully. "I'll slow the speed," he said. "That's all I'm allowed to do. You try to get somebody to see us."

Duffy stood up, spread the skirt with her palms. She waved at the windows and lamps and lights as they went by. The dress was red. She wavered to keep from falling overboard, threw out both arms, and yelled, and on both sides the towns and cities of the earth drove by.

The
Mother-in-Law

$$\neq$$

I cross the alley which runs between the back of the neighborhood grocery and the back of *her* house. I believe it is 1932. Now softly to the lighted bedroom window to part the dry spirea twigs and see through the cloudy pane.

Already yellowing, she rests in the high bed and breathes through her mouth. She is barely forty and her heart does not want to stop; it beats against the cancer like a fist on a landslide.

They sit around her bed. Husband, three sons. Another long evening. They talk over the day like any ordinary family.

There is the youngest boy, Philip. Black eyes and silence. In ten more years, he will marry me.

She does not ask them the only question which still concerns her: Will you look after Ross? So they do not answer. If I could slip into the room and make her hear, I would whisper, "Yes, of course"; but she has never heard of me, and never will.

I am a ghost here and my other self is skipping rope in another state.

* * *

Snow on the alley. Nathan, the eldest, hangs back. He feels responsible for everything he sees, and started living through a long lens at an early age. Ahead of him, Ross is scraping fingers in the snow, slinging handfuls behind him. My future husband walks sideways, so he can look ahead and watch Ross at the same time. He lacks Nathan's sense of duty; with him, all is instinct.

They come to the rear of the grocery store, where trucks unload at the ramp and fermenting produce is piled in cans. Since the woolen mill closed, the cans rattle all night. People trot up the alley carrying tow sacks.

With his good arm, Ross makes a snowball spatter on their empty garage. The car has been sold. Nathan tries to decide whether the thump disturbs their mother. My husband throws snow, too, and makes his ball fall short. By instinct.

Nathan stops, points. Above the loading ramp, the grocer has installed two poles with electric lights which will shine directly on the garbage cans. Now the boys must keep their window shades pulled at night to avoid recognizing the fathers of friends.

They turn in the sagging wire gate to their backyard. Under the snow lie *her* crowded iris; the stalks of uncut chrysanthemums rattle when Ross limps through. Nathan reaches out to help him across a drift. Before he can grasp the hand, my future husband has dropped snow down Ross's back; they roll and tussle. Philip gets wetter. A draw—Ross laughs. I am watching the scene with my own hand out; if I were to change this or that?

They walk through my transparent arm and climb the back steps. The pattern is set.

* * *

Mr. Felts has asked the grocer not to burn his big lights all night long. "They shine in her window." She sleeps so little now, even with medicine. All night he hears the "sooo—soooo" as she sucks breath through her clenched teeth.

The grocer says the police advised it. His windows, door locks are being broken. Obliquely he blames Mr. Felts for the Depression, because he is an accountant and is still working the town's math when its weaving machines have stopped.

The grocer's son ran a machine. "I better leave them on."

Mr. Felts fastens her window shade with thumbtacks. Still the gold leaks in. The shine frightens her; she knows the back alley has never been bright. If there is a fire, Ross will not be able to get away.

Again Mr. Felts begs the grocer. Those who raid the garbage cans do it hastily now, half blinded, in a clatter. She hears; she sucks air faster. One night a metal lid rolls down the entire alley and spins out with a twang against the corner curb. She—who never missed church until this illness—cries out about Ezekiel's chariot.

Next morning, in full sight of the neighborhood, Mr. Felts heaves bricks at the light until both bulbs are broken. He wants to throw one at the grocer, too, but Nathan stops him.

March. When they come home from the funeral, Ross hurries to the bedroom. He does not understand she will not lie there anymore. Only Nathan was old enough to see inside the box. He takes Ross now onto the back steps and speaks for a long time about death and Heaven. Ross hits him.

In her bedroom, their father pulls outward gently on the shade. One by one, the thumbtacks pop onto the floor like buttons off a fat man. My husband smiles when he sees this; my ghost smiles. How I am going to love him!

Crying at last, Ross slams the back door and screams his name.

"Come here," Philip says. "Help me pick up these tacks."

Ross was born with a bad arm and leg. One eye is fixed and useless; there is slight vision in the other. While there was money, the Feltses saw many doctors. Casts and splints were used; his night brace banged the bars of the crib when he dreamed.

His spectacles are plain glass and thick glass, so his brain seems to be bulging out through the magnified eye which strains to see shapes, light, and shadow. Ross is intelligent and, thanks to *her*, well adjusted. She must have bitten her tongue half off the day he climbed onto the garage roof. How her throat swelled shut the first of the hundred times he fell downstairs. But she was successful. All boys fall, Ross thinks.

Summer evenings there was baseball in the vacant lot by the grocer's. Ross batted like a spider, ran bases like a crab. The boys' laughter sounded to him like comradeship. In the bull pen Nathan made sure it was. Philip told me these things.

Now that I have Philip's children, I know how many bloody noses she iced in the pantry. I go into that pantry and watch her from behind the flour bin. She is thinking about the first lumps which have bent her nipple. I understand why she's sure they are harmless; it is not her *turn* for cancer. At night I tap my foot silently by the green chair while she searches her Bible. I'm not a Bible reader myself. I like the Greek myths. She reads St. Paul.

Staring at the green chair, where in more than a decade my other self will sit, she almost meets my eyes, almost pledges to accept any unbeliever who will care for Ross.

"I'm going to be pretty and red-haired," I say—she doesn't care.

"In bed, Philip and I . . ." She can't be bothered.

She dreams beyond me of how Ross kicked against her womb with a foot that could not have been withered. It was Achilles' foot.

Nathan, the dutiful son, has brought her daisies, which she puts absently into a vase. I beg her: Look at my Philip now. He carries no flowers but his black eyes—does she see? Now she embraces Ross and, over his crooked shoulder, gazes deeply at her other sons. She cannot help it; she has begun to bargain. Will they? Can they? Has she prepared them to?

Harmless as marbles, the fragments of her death shift in her breast and another, smaller, rolls in the womb that sheltered Ross and the others. I, Nathan's wife, their children, ours—we hear the bits roll as she looks through time and our faces.

She lets Ross go; the moment passes, will exist in no one's memory but hers and mine.

In 1942, Nathan becomes an army officer. Philip is in high school, unaware that in another state I am in love with a basketball center who owns his own car. We park in it, too; I evade his long arms. Philip's ghost sits in the backseat. I sense him there. I am uneasy, dimly suspecting he exists, fearing his shade is nothing but my frigidity.

This is the year Mr. Felts has almost finished paying the cost of her futile treatment—X rays and pills—the headstone. He shrinks as the bills shrink; his flesh seems to drain away toward hers. Philip says, "You rest, I'll read tonight." Ross is a college freshman. They take turns with his texts.

The grocery store has been torn down and a warehouse built. Its lights shine day and night, and light up the place in her yard where the iris roots have reared up to lie on the ground like a tumble of potatoes.

At fifteen, I go away to girls' camp in the Blue Ridge Mountains. My parents can afford it. Across the same lake, their church holds summer retreat. Mr. Felts has brought the two younger boys because he promised her. In the dark, Philip smokes secretly after hours and stares over the black water at the lights of the camp where I am sleeping. I can't see what Mr. Felts is doing.

Once, on my horse, I ride across the place where Philip and Ross have had a picnic; they have just gone; maybe no more than a rhododendron bush keeps us from meeting.

Up the hill as they walk away, Ross is asking, "Isn't it time you got interested in girls?"

Now it's time. I go to college in his town. I am eighteen, so ignorant and idealistic that the qualities overlap and blend. My grades are good. I think I will become a social worker and improve the world. I sign up to read to blind students.

(Here I must pause. The ghost of my English teacher protests such melodrama, such coincidence. I, too, protest it. I am a tool of the plot, a flat character rung in on the proper page. I say—with Iphigenia—thanks but no thanks! The blade comes on.)

In no time at all, I move from knowing Ross to knowing Philip. I recognize him. He looks like his mother. While we are falling in love, we take Ross everywhere with us. He can ride a gentle mare, swim in an awkward backstroke. In the balcony, we explain movie scenes if the dialogue is vague. He hardly notices when we kiss or touch each other. One night, drunk and tired of trying to work out marriage plans, we let Ross drive down a country road—screaming directions, "Right!" and "Left!"—till all three of us hurt from laughing. I kiss Philip so hard my own teeth bite me.

Secretly, Ross talks to me about wanting girls. I repeat it to Philip, whose black eyes go blacker. Nathan is mailing long letters home about how Ross should save himself for his bride.

In spite of what the basketball center said, I am not frigid. Lost at last under Philip, Philip lost in me. In the silence afterward, the ghost of Ross. We get up and dress and go find him and take him for a long walk. Coming home, we sit with our backs against the warehouse, singing. Soprano, tenor, baritone, under the blazing lights.

We marry and the war ends. Ross has a job running a machine he can pedal with one foot. With his checks he buys radios and phonographs. Every morning, Mr. Felts cooks him Cream of Wheat.

Philip and I live over a beauty shop. The smell of hot hair has got into our linens. Philip finishes college; Nathan comes home and begins.

Saturday nights I go to her house and cook a big pot of spaghetti. I am pregnant with our first. Philip is independent and we have refused to cash my parents' checks, which have grown smaller anyway.

I wash the dishes in her sink. Did she cook spaghetti here? Ross likes it. Yes.

Late in the evening when my back aches, I leave the men talking and lie across her bed. They have painted the windowsill, but its frame is neatly pocked where the shade was nailed down. I lie there fearful for my child. I ask her: What were the earliest signs? Did you vomit much? Take vitamins? But she has slipped into the room where Ross and the others are playing cards.

Our daughter is almost ready for kindergarten. The next one is walking and throwing toys; the third sleeps through the night at last. I have got used to the beauty-shop smell.

The telephone rings. Ross says, "I came in? The coffee wasn't fixed?"

I call to our bedroom, "Philip?"

In my ear the telephone: "I can't find where he's gone."

"I'll come," Philip says.

They find Mr. Felts in the furnace room. The shovel is under the coal, and he has gone down around its handle like a wilted vine. His heart tried to get out; all is stained.

We bring Ross home to our four rooms. Afterward I visit her empty house. Where are you, Mr. Felts? What was it like for you? Why did you never say?

Silence. He was as still as Philip is.

Ross lives with us now. Nathan fills out his income tax. He buys insurance policies for Ross. He never forgets a birthday and they ask Ross to dinner once a month. Nathan's daughters go to orthodontists and reducing salons.

I carry four baskets of laundry up these stairs instead of three. Our children like bread pudding. All four are healthy, make noise, eat a lot. They will have straighter teeth when the second set comes in.

Philip works too hard. Some Saturday nights he sits in the kitchen and drinks whiskey alone until his own limbs seem crippled. I have to help him down the hall. "Something worrying you?"

"What could be worrying me?"

I have stopped asking. What he cannot say, I must not. Mostly we talk over our days like any ordinary family.

Sometimes when our bedspring has stopped squeaking, I can hear Ross's squeak. Do the children hear? What will we do when they are too old to share his room? He never complains of the sweat when the vaporizer steams all night and I come in and out with aspirin. Sometimes he sits up in bed to smoke and wait. I'm afraid he'll set the mattress afire some night when I sleep through the smoke.

"Let me light you a cigarette," he always offers.

I always let him. Philip says Ross needs to give us something back.

Lung cancer? I never say that aloud. Secretly, I flush the butt down the toilet.

"I've got more," Ross always calls pleasantly when I come back into the hall.

Now, while the children sleep and Ross sleeps among them and I sit down at last to wait for Philip to come from his overtime work, somebody rattles my garbage can; somebody breathes on my glass, looking in. Somebody's glance like a blaze of light gets under my shade.

I am mending *his* shirt. I am forty, like *her.*

I say to the black windowpane: Yes, we are. Go away.

She understands and her gaze burns past to where Ross still sleeps in a brace in the crib she bought. I understand her, too. Even on weary nights, I am glad her desire found me, drew me to this room.

He's just fine, I say. He will live a long life.

Then, for one icy moment, the ghost of her envy stares at the ghost of mine.

Beasts of the Southern Wild

. . . I have been in this prison a long time, years, since the Revolution. They have made me an animal. They drive us in and out our cells like cattle to stalls. Our elbows and knees are jagged and our legs and armpits swarm with hair.

We are all women, all white, bleached whiter now and sickly as blind moles. All our jailers, of course, are black.

So much has been done to us that we are bored with everything, and when they march me and six others to the Choosing Room, we make jokes about it and bark with laughter. I am too old to be chosen—thirty when I came. And now? Two hundred. It is not clear to me what has happened to my husband and my sons. Like a caged chicken on a truck, I have forgotten the cock and the fledglings.

We file into the Choosing Room and from dim instinct stand straighter on the concrete floors and lift our sharp chins. The Chooser sits on an iron stool. Negro, of course, in his forties, rich, his hair like a halo that burned down to twisted cinders. Jim Brown used to look like him; there's a touch of Sidney Poitier—but he has thin lips. I insist on that: thin lips.

They line us up and he paces out of sight to examine our ankles and haunches. He will choose Wilma, no doubt, who still has some shape to her and whose hair is yellow.

The Chooser steps back to his seat and picks up our stacked files and asks the guard a few soft questions while a brown finger is pointed at first this one of us and then that. This procedure is unusual. The dossiers are always there, containing every detail of our past lives. Usually they are consulted only after the field has been narrowed and two finalists checked for general health, sound teeth.

He speaks to the guard, who looks surprised, then beckons to me. The others, grumbling, are herded out and I am left standing in front of the Chooser. He is very tall. I say to his throat, "Why me?" He taps my dossier against some invisible surface in the air and goes out to sign my contract.

"You're lucky," says the guard through his thick lips.

I am beginning to be afraid. That's strange. I've been beaten now, been raped, other things. These are routine. But something will change now and I fear any changes. I ask who the man is who will take me to his house for whatever use he wants, and the guard says, "Sam Porter." He takes me out a side door and puts me in the backseat of a long car and tells me to be quiet and not move around. And I wait for Sam Porter like a mongrel bitch he has bought from the pound.

When the alarm clock rang, she dragged herself upright and hung on to the bookcase. She loved to sleep—a few more seconds prone and she'd be gone again, with the whole family late for work and school. She balanced on one foot and kicked Rob lightly in the calf. "Up, Rob. Rob? Up!"

Fry bacon, cook oatmeal, scramble eggs, make coffee. There was a tiny box, transistorized, under her mastoid bone.

All day long it gave her orders, and between times it hummed like a tuning fork deep in her ear. Set table. Bring in milk and newspaper. Spoons, forks. Sugar bowl, cream.

She yelled, "Breakfast!"

Nobody came and the shower was still running. Down the hall both boys quarreled over who got to keep the pencil with the eraser. When the shower stopped, she yelled again, "Breakfast!" (I'm Rob's transistor box.)

Her husband and sons came in and ate. Grease, toast, crumbs, wet rings on the table. Egg yolk running on one plate, a liquefied eye. If thine eye offend thee, pluck it out.

"Don't forget my money," Michael said, and Robbie, "Me, too."

"How much you need?" She counted out lunch money, a subscription to *Weekly Reader*. Rob said he'd leave the clothes at the cleaners, patted her, and went off to the upholstery shop. She drove the boys to school, then across town to the larger one where she taught English, Grade 12, which she liked, and Girls' Hygiene, which she despised. It was November, and the girls endured nutrition charts only because they could look ahead to a chapter on human reproduction the class should reach before Christmas.

Today's lesson was on the Seven Basic Foods, and one smart-mouth, as usual, had done her essay on eating all of one type each day, then balancing the diet in weekly blocks. The girl droned her system aloud to the class. "So on Wednesday we indulge in the health-giving green and yellow vegetables group, which may be prepared in astonishing variety, from appetizing salads to delicious soups to assorted nourishing casseroles."

None of the students would use a short word when three long ones would do. They loved hyperbole. Carol Walsh wanted to say, "There's no variety, none at all," but this was not part of their education. She was very sleepy. When she looked with half-closed eyes out the schoolroom window, the landscape billowed like a silk tapestry and its folds blew back in her face like colored veils.

In the hall later, a student asked, "Miz Walsh? What kind of essay you want on Coleridge? His life and all?"

"No, no. His poetry."

"I can't find much on his poetry." The boy was bug-eyed and gasping, helpless as a fish. Couldn't find some library book to tell him in order what each line of the poems *meant.*

She said, "Just think about the poems, George. Experience them. Use your imagination." Flap your wings, little fish. She went into English class depressed. There was nothing to see out this window but a wall of concrete blocks and, blurred, it looked like a dirty sponge.

"Before we move to today's classwork, I'm getting questions about your Coleridge essay. I'm not interested in a record of the man's biography. I don't even want a paper on what kind of poet he might have been without an opium addiction." A flicker of interest in the back row. "I want you to react to the poems, emotionally. To do what Coleridge did, put your emphasis on imagination and sensibility, not just reason." She saw the film drop over thirty-five gazes, like the extra eyelids of thirty-five reptiles. "Mood, feeling," she said. The class was integrated, and boredom did the same thing to a black face as to a white.

The Potter girl raised her hand. "I've done a special project on Coleridge and I wondered if that would count instead?"

Count, count. They came to her straight from math and waited for the logarithms of poetry. Measure me, Miz Walsh. Am I sufficient?

She said, "See me after class, Ann. Now, everybody, turn in your text to the seven poems you read by Thomas Lovell Beddoes." They whispered and craned in their desks, although the section had been assigned for homework. Dryly she said, "Page 309. First of all, against the definition we've been using for the past section, is Beddoes a romantic poet?"

Evelina dropped one choked laugh like a porpoise under water. Romantic, for her, had only one definition.

"Ralph?"

Ralph dragged one shoe on the floor and stared at the scrape it left. "Sort of in between." His heel rasped harder when she asked why. "He was born later? There's a lot of nature in his poems, though." He studied her face for clues. "But not as much as Wordsworth?"

His girlfriend raised her hand quickly to save him and blurted, "I like the one that goes, 'If there were dreams to sell,/What would you buy?' " In the back, one of the boys made soft, mock-vomit noises in his throat.

After class Ann Potter carried to the front of the room and unrolled on the desk a poster of a huge tree painted in watercolor. Its roots were buried in the soil of Classicism and Neoclassicism; "18th Century," it said in a black parenthesis. Dryden, Swift, and Pope had been written in amongst the root tangle. James Thomson vertically on the rising trunk. Then there were thick limbs branching off assigned to Keats, Shelley, Byron. . . .

When Ann smiled, she showed two even rows of her orthodontist's teeth. "This sort of says it all, doesn't it, Miz Walsh!"

"You could probably be a very successful public schoolteacher."

"It's got dates and everything."

"Everything." Blake's *Songs of Innocence* branched off to

one side, where Byron would not be scraped in a high wind. "Tintern Abbey." There was a whole twig allotted to "Kubla Khan."

"I thought you might count this equal to a term paper, Miz Walsh. I mean, I had to look things up. I spent just days on it."

"Ann, why not write the paper anyway? Then this can be extra credit if you need it." She'd need it. There was nothing in her skull but filtered air, stored in a meticulous honeycomb.

"My talents lie more in art, I think. I had to mix and mix to get just that shade of green, since England's a green country. I read that someplace. The Emerald Isle and all. I read a lot."

"It's a very attractive tree."

For last period, Carol Walsh gave a writing assignment; they could keep their textbooks open. Compare Beddoes and Southey. She sat at her desk making bets with herself about how many first sentences would state when each man was born. I'm good at dates, Miz Walsh. That Poe *looks* crazy. Well, Blake had this vision of a tiger, burning bright. He was this visionary. And he wrote this prayer about it.

That night she graded health tests until she herself could hardly remember what part of the digestive tract ran into what other part and whether the small or the large intestine came first. She chewed up an apple as she worked, half expecting its residue to drop, digested, out her left ear. Who knew what a forbidden fruit might take it in its—in *her* head to do?

"You're going to bed this early?" Rob glanced up from the magazine he was skimming during TV commercials.

"Not to sleep. Just to rest my eyes. Leave the TV on. I might decide to watch that movie." She got into bed and immediately curled up facing the wall. She was drowsy but curious, not ready for sleep; and there was nothing on television to compare with the pictures she could make herself. The apple had left her teeth feeling tender, and she had munched out the pulp from every dark seed, cyanide and all. Once she'd read of a man who loved apple seeds and saved up a cupful for a feast and it killed him.

She smiled when the story started.

. . . The car is moving. Its chauffeur is white, a free white who could buy off his contract. Sam Porter has said nothing. He does not even look at me but out the window. For years I have seen no city streets and I long to get off the floor and look, too; but he might strike me with that cane. A black cane, very slim, with a knob of jasper. The tops of buildings glimpsed do not look new. It's hard to rebuild after revolutions.

We stop at last. I follow him through a narrow gate, bordered with a clipped yew hedge. A town house, narrow and high, like the ones they used to build in Charleston. This one is blue. A white man is raking in the tulip beds—spring, then. I had forgotten. Sam Porter walks straight through the foyer and up the stairs and shows me a bedroom. "Clean up and dress." He opens a closet with many dresses, walks through a bathroom and out a door on the far side. So. Our rooms adjoin. Mine seems luxurious.

I do not look at myself until I am deep in the soapy water. My body is a ruin. No breasts at all. I can rake one fingernail down my ribs as if along a picket fence. The flesh which remains on my legs is strung there, loose, like a curtain swag. I am crying. I soak my head but lice do not drown; and finally I find a shampoo he has left for me which makes them float on the water and speckle the ring around the tub. I scrub it and wash myself again.

The dresses are made of soft material, folded crêpes and draped jerseys, and I do not look so thin in the red one, although it turns my face white as a china plate. He may prefer that. I wonder if there is a Mrs. Porter; I hope not. They have grown delicate since the war and faint easily and some of the prison women have been poisoned by them. I pin up my wet hair and redden my lips, so thin now I no longer have a mouth, only a hole in my jaw. He knocks on the door. "We'll eat. Downstairs." His voice is very deep. I have lived so long with the voices of women that his sound makes a bass vibration on my skin.

Practicing the feel of shoes again, I go down alone to find him. The table is large, linen-covered. I am set at his right. There's soup and a wine. It's hard not to dribble. The white housekeeper changes our plates for fish and a new wine. She looks at me with pity. She must be sixty-five. Where is my mother keeping house? At what tables do my sisters sit tonight?

"Carol Walsh," he says suddenly, looking down as if he can read me off his tablecloth.

The wine has changed me. "Sam Porter," I say in the same tone, to surprise him. He lifts his face and his forehead glistens from heat on its underside. His eyes are larger than mine, wetter, even the tiny veins seem brown.

"What do you expect of me?" I ask, but he shakes his head and begins eating the pale fish meat. I put it in my mouth and it disappears. Only the sweet taste but no bulk, and I am hungry, hungry.

After dinner he waves one hand and I follow him to a sitting room with bookshelves and dark walls. "Your file indicates you are literate, a former English teacher." He has no trouble taking down a book from a very high shelf. "Read to me. Your choice."

I choose Yeats. I choose "Innisfree" and "Sleuth Wood." To him I read aloud: "Be secret and exult/Because of all things known/That is most difficult." He sits in his big chair listening, a cold blue ring on his finger. I turn two pages and read, "Sailing to Byzantium."

When that is done, Sam Porter says, "What poem did you skip? And why?"

I have hurried past the page which has "Leda and the Swan." The lines are in my head but I cannot read them here: ". . . the staggering girl, her thighs caressed/By the dark webs . . ."

I say aloud, "I'll go back and read it, then," but the poem I substitute is "Coole Park," and he knows; he knows. He smiles in his chair and offers me brandy, which turns my sweat gold. He says, "You look well."

"Not yet. I look old and fresh from prison."

He rises, very tall, and does not look at me. "Shall we go up?"

I follow on the stairs, watching his thighs when he lifts each leg, how the muscles catch. He passes through my room and I follow; but he stops at the door to his and shakes his frizzed head. "When you come to me," he says, "it will not be with your shoulders squared."

He closes the door while I am still saying "Thank you." I cannot even tell if what I feel is gratitude or disappointment.

They drove Sunday afternoon to look at a new house in the town's latest subdivision. "Wipe your feet, boys," said Carol. The foyer was tiled with marbleized vinyl, and in the wallpaper mural a bird—half Japanese and half Virginian—flew over bonsai magnolias.

"If the interest rates weren't so damn high," Rob said, muffled in a closet. "That's one more thing George Wallace would have done. Cut down that interest."

"It's got a fireplace. Boys, stay off those steps. They don't have a railing yet."

"Bedrooms are mighty little. Not much way to add on, either. Maybe the basement can be converted."

There were already plastic logs in the fireplace and a jet for a gas flame. Their furniture, all of it old and recovered by Rob's upholsterers, seemed too wide to go through the doorways. He called to her from the kitchen, "Built-in appliances!" She could see the first plaster crack above the corner of the kitchen door. Rob had gone down into the basement and yelled for them to stay out, too many nails and lumber piles. "Lots of room, though," called his hollow voice. "I could have myself a little shop. Build a rumpus room?"

Carol stood in the kitchen turning faucets on and off—though there were no water lines to the house yet—and clicking the wall switches that gave no light. I could get old here, in this house. Stand by this same sink when I'm forty and fifty and sixty. Die in that airtight bedroom with its cedar closets when I'm eighty-two. By the time they roll me out the front walk, the boxwoods will be high.

"Drink of water?"

"Not working, Robbie. See?"

"Well, Michael peed in the toilet!"

"It'll evaporate," she said. They were handsome boys, and Robbie was bright. Michael had been slower to talk and slower to read; nothing bothered him. Robbie was born angry and had stayed angry most of his life. Toys broke for him;

66

brothers tattled; bicycles threw boys on gravel. Balls flew past his waiting glove. Robbie could think up a beautiful picture and the crayons ruined it. She'd say to him, "Thinking's what matters," and doubt if that were true.

"We move in this house, I want a room by myself," he announced now, and punched at the hanging light fixture. "Michael's a baby. Michael wets in the bed."

In the doorway Michael stretched his face with all fingers and stuck out his dripping tongue and roared for the fun of it.

"Michael gets in my things all the time. He marked up my zoo book. He tore the giraffe."

Rob's head rose out of the stairwell. "No harm in asking the price and what kind of mortgage deal we could get. You agree, Carol? It's got a big backyard. We could build a fence."

"Could we get a dog?" Michael yelled.

Robbie pinched his arm. "I want my own dog. I want a big dog with teeth. I'll keep him in my room to bite you if you come in messing things up."

Carol made both boys be quiet, and in the car agreed the house was far better than the one they rented now. Rob smiled and swung the wheel easily, as if the car were an extension of his body, something he wore about him like a familiar harness.

"I like that smell of raw wood and paint," he said. "Yesterday we had a nigger couch to cover, a fold-out couch, and it smelled so bad Pete moved it in the back lot and tore it down out there. Beats me why they smell different. It's in the sweat, I guess."

Robbie was listening hard from the backseat, and she was afraid tomorrow he would be sniffing around his school's only Negro teacher. "There's no difference," she said, putting her elbow deep in Rob's side.

"You college people kill me."

They drove in silence while she set up in her mind two columns: His thoughts and Hers. He was thinking how tired he was of a know-it-all wife, who'd have been an old maid if Rob Walsh hadn't come along, a prize, a real catch. With half-interest in his daddy's business just waiting for them. Gave Carol everything, and still she stayed snooty. Didn't drink, didn't gamble, didn't chase women—but by God he might! He might yet! He was two years younger. He was better-looking. He didn't have to keep on with this Snow Queen here, with Miss Icebox. Old Frosty Brain, Frozen Ass. Who needed it?

And Her thoughts, accusing. Who do I think I am? What options did I ever have? Was I beautiful, popular, a genius? Once when we quarreled, Rob said to me, "Hell, you've been in menopause since you were twenty." I'll never forgive him for that. For being mediocre, maybe; but never for saying that.

Turning into their driveway, Rob said in a sullen voice, "You college people can't be bothered believing your noses. All you believe is books." He got out of the car and went into the house and left them sitting there.

Robbie said to his brother, "I warned you not to pee in that toilet."

After supper of leftover roast, Carol read the boys another chapter from *Winnie the Pooh*. When she had heard their flippant prayers and turned out the light, she stood in the hall and smiled as they whispered from bed to bed. I can love them till my ribs ache, but it still seems like an afterthought. She dreaded to go downstairs and watch the cowboys fight each other on a little screen, one in the white hat, one in the black.

While she was ironing Rob a clean work shirt for tomorrow, she wondered if there were some way she could ask Sam Porter about an odor without offending him. She decided against it.

. . . I have been here two weeks and Sam has never laid a hand on me. Yet I am treated like a favorite concubine. I dine at his table; he dresses me as though the sight of me gave him pleasure. The housekeeper mourns over what she imagines of our nights together. Every evening, I read to him—one night he asked for Othello *just to laugh at my startled face. One other evening, he had friends over and made me play hostess from a corner chair. He encouraged me to join in the talk, which was of new writers unknown to me. One of the men—a runt with a chimpanzee's face—looked me over as if I might be proffered to him along with the cigars. Plainly, he could do better on his own. He made one harem joke, a coarse one, and jerked his thumb toward me and up. Sam Porter tapped him atop his spine. "Not in my house," he said. I was looking away, grinding my teeth. To me he said, "Sit straight. There's nothing in your contract which says. . . . Some things you need not endure."*

"He isn't worth my anger." Sam laughed, but the others worried and took him off in the front hall to offer advice.

Tonight as we sit down with our brandy, he says to me, "You were happy in the old days? As a woman?"

"Sometimes."

"My color and hair. Perhaps they disgust you?"

"No. Although in prison we were often . . . forced. I cannot forget those times."

"And you never had pleasure? From a black?"

"No. None. What shall I read tonight?"

"From yourself, perhaps? Or the women prisoners?"

"Not much," I say quickly, and, "Should we read some of the new things your friends like?"

"What subject did you choose for your Master's thesis?"

By now I know Sam Porter is no quick-rich, quick-cultured black. He is Provost at New Africa University, which I attended under its old name. And my dusty thesis must be stored there, in the prewar stacks. If he wished to know my subject, then he already knows it. I answer truthfully anyway, "John Donne."

He hands me a book of collected writings, from the library at school. "Perhaps the early work?" I reach for it and my fingers graze his. His hand is warmer than mine—unscientific, I know; but I can feel old sunlight pooled in his flesh and my hand feels wintry by his.

I am sorry to have the book again. The blue veins on my hands are high as the runs of moles; when I held Donne last, I had no veins at all and my skin was soft. I was twenty-three then, and not in menopause. No! I felt isolated from all things and swollen with myself as a tree hangs ripe with unplucked fruit. I was ugly, if the young are ever ugly; and sat alone in the caves and tunnels of the library, at a desk heaped high with Donne's mandrake root. Sam Porter says, "When you tire of staring at the cover, perhaps you will read?"

"The Sunne Rising." I look to a different page and, perversely, read aloud, "I can love both faire and browne/Her whom abundance melts and her whom want betraies."

Sam is watching me; I feel it though I do not look up. Sometimes his eye lens seems wide as a big cat's, and it magnifies the light and throws it in perforations onto me. I swallow, read, "Her who loves lonenesse best, and her who maskes and *plaies.*" My voice is thin through my dry mouth. I ask Donne's question, "Will it not serve your turn to do, as did your mothers?/Or have you all vices spent, and now would finde out others?/Or doth a feare, that men are true, torment you?"

When the poem is done, there is silence. He drinks his brandy; I drink mine; is it as warm going down inside him as in me? His glass clicks on the table. "You sit awhile. The brandy's there, and the book. I'm tired tonight."

I sit numb in my chair. He passes, then, with one swoop, bends down and touches my mouth with his, and his lips are not thin—not thin at all. He walks out quickly and I sit with the book and the snifter tight in my hands, for there is a smell; yes, it is sweetish, like a wilted carnation fermenting on an August grave. Even a mouthful of brandy does not wash out his scent. My lungs are rich with it. And I do not go upstairs for a long time, until Sam Porter is asleep in the other room.

All evening she had been marking the participles which hung loose in the Coleridge essays like rags; and all evening Rob kept interrupting her work. He talked of the new house and what their monthly payments would be if they took a ten-year mortgage, or twenty. Or thirty—like a judge considering sentence.

"I'm leaving that up to you," she said, trying to figure out on which page Ann Potter had changed Kubla Khan to Genghis Khan in her paper, "The Tree of Romanticism."

Rob said if she'd give less written work she wouldn't have to waste so much time marking papers. One of the themes— George's—appeared to be copied from an encyclopedia. Symptoms of opiate intoxication. There followed a list of Coleridge's poems. "These," George wrote, "show clearly the effects of the drug on his mind." She turned the page but there wasn't a word more.

Rob said, "If the federal government would just quit raising the minimum wage. How can I tell how much I'll earn in a year or two years, the way they eat into profits more and more? You know how much I got to pay a guy just to put chairs on a truck and drive them across town?"

"Umm." Ralph's paper was "Nature in Wordsworth and Coleridge" and how Wordsworth had more of it and wrote prettier.

"The harder I work, the more I send to Washington to keep some shiftless s.o.b. drawing welfare," Rob said, and rattled his newspaper. "And next year they raise my taxes to build back the big cities the bums are burning down. So everybody can draw welfare in new buildings, for Christ's sake. My daddy would turn over in his grave."

There's life, she thought, in the old boy yet. She read an essay on an albatross, a harmless bird feeding on fish and squid, and no need for anybody to fear it.

Rob was asleep when she marked the last red-letter grades and slipped between the sheets like an otter going under the surface without a ripple. She lay wide-eyed in the dark. The streetlight shone through the window blinds, and threw stripes across their bed and her face. After a while she slid one hand under the covers and closed her eyes.

. . . Sam is sick. The doctor who came was the chimpanzee man and he pinched in the air at me—but I moved. There is something of me to pinch now, after Sam's food and his wines and my long, lazy days in his handsome house. The doctor says he has flu, not serious; and for two days I have been giving him capsules and citrus juices. The housekeeper sees I am worried

and has lost all her pity. She turns her face from me when I draw near, as if my gaze would leave a permanent stain. Last night I sat by his bed and read to him:

> *"Are Sunne, Moone, or Starres by law forbidden*
> *To smile where they list, or lend away their light?*
> *Are birds divorc'd, or are they chidden*
> *If they leave their mate, or lie abroad a-night?"*

He fell asleep from his fever and I read alone and sometimes laid my hand on his blazing forehead. Against his color, my hand had more shape and weight than it has ever had.

Tonight he is much better and sips hot lemonade and listens with half his attention to old favorites. "Come live with me and be my love."

He asks once, "You don't sing, do you?"

"No."

He falls asleep. I tiptoe into my own room. Perhaps in the Choosing Room there is someone new, who sings. I pace on my carpet, John Donne's poems open on my dressing table like a snare. He hooks me with his frayed old line, "For thee, thou needst no such deceit/For thou thy selfe art thine owne bait." I close the book; I spring his trap; I leap away.

In the mirror I see who I really am . . . my hair grown long and brown, my eyes brown, my skin toasted by the sun on Sam Porter's noonday roof. I will never be pretty, but this is the closest I have ever come, and I pinch my own cheeks and look at myself sideways. I have grown round again from eating at his table, and my breasts are distended with his brandy. I put on the red robe and walk softly into the next room. Sam sleeps, turned away from me, with one dark hand half open on the pillow as if something should alight in it.

I return to my room and brush out my hair. My body has a

foreign fragrance—perhaps from these bottles and creams. Perhaps I absorb it from the air.

I pass through to the next room and drop my robe on the floor. I turn off the lamp and he is darker than the room. I slide in against his back, the whole length of him hot from fever. I reach around to hold him in my right hand. He is soft as flowers. He makes some sound and stirs; then he lies still and I feel wakefulness rise in him and his skin prickles. He turns; his arms are out. I am taken into his warm darkness and lie in the lion's mouth.

The bed shook and she opened her eyes and stared at the luminous face of the clock. Rob said, "You asleep?" She lay very still, breathing deep and careful, pressing her hand tight between her thighs as if to hold back an outcry. The air was thick with Old Spice shaving lotion—a bad sign. A hand struck her hip like a flyswatter. "Carol? You can't be asleep." The ghostly face of the clock showed 1 A.M. "Honey?"

She jerked her hand free just in time for his. "Ah," he said with satisfaction against her shoulder blades. He curled around her from behind. "Picked a good time, huh?" She moved obediently so it would be quickly done, and he rolled away from her and slept with one arm over hers like a weighted chain.

. . . Sam bends over the bed where I have been crying and now lie weary, past crying. "Who was it, Carol? Tell me who it was?"

I roll my head away from him and he kisses one damp temple, then the other. He whispers, "This isn't prison anymore, hear me, Carol? No more endurance is required. Understand that. You are home, here; and that was rape. Whoever it was, I'll punish him."

I am a single bruise. "No." I run my hand under his shirt. "I didn't encourage him, Sam, I didn't. He broke in here—I was alone. I called for you. I never wanted him."

"If you do," says Sam, "I'll tear up your contract and let you go."

"No." I look in his eyes. "He was never my desire. An intruder. A thief. He forced himself on me. I swear it."

"Tell me one thing." He lies by me and his heat comes through the blanket. "Was he a white man?"

"Yes. He was white."

Gently he holds me, says, "I can have him killed, then. You know that. Did you know him?"

"I know his name. That's all we know, each other's names."

His hair is black and jumbled. "If you tell me his name, I can have him killed. But I won't ask you to do that. You must choose. You'll not be blamed if you choose silence." His hands are so pale on one side, so dark on the other.

"Rob Walsh," I whisper. "Rob Walsh."

"We'll hunt him down," he says, and gets up and goes downstairs.

He does not come back for hours and I wake near dawn to see him stripping off the black suit, the black mask, the black cloak. I sit up in bed. "It's done," he says, sounding tired, maybe sick. He comes naked and curly to me and falls away on the far side. "There's no love left in me tonight."

But I am there, my hands busy, and I can devour him; he will yield to me. The room is dark and he is so dark, and all I can see is the running back and forth of my busy hands, like pale spiders who have lived underground too long.

Burning the Bed

Isabel tapped lightly on her brakes to keep from ramming the long ambulance which was bringing her father home. Its taillights winked and the painted cross on the rear doors swayed down the clay road which had washed ragged with winter rains, then frozen in lumps and craters. Now the last snow had sunk into the soil. The mud was cold, rust-colored.

Isabel rolled down her car window, leaned out, pressed her horn. The ambulance turned left. One minute, Isabel thought. That's all it would take to check the mailbox. It seemed to her the aluminum door was cracked, that even as she drove by something white with her name on it could be seen. She braked harder, and the rear wheels floated slightly to one side on the slick mud.

"Goddamnit," she said aloud, pulling into the ruts left by the ambulance. She'd probably have to walk back for her letter, through the mire and after dark.

While she parked in the far corner of the yard, the hospital driver rocked back and forth, then swung in a slippery crescent and backed toward the front steps. Both attendants got out, opened the ambulance doors. Then they looked toward her car.

"I'm coming," Isabel said. She put her key ring in her pocketbook next to Brenda's postcard. She checked the hand brake.

When she was halfway to the house, the driver said, "If you'll just hold open the front door." Isabel did not like his tone.

Into the ambulance the other man said, "Get you right inside, Mr. Perkins." They slid him out as carefully as a pane of glass. Isabel was looking down at his head. A skull thrust through his face.

"How deep was the snow?" he said to them all. His smile looked raw. Isabel was carrying his false teeth in her pocketbook.

"You rest, Papa."

"A couple of inches." The orderly moved to the foot of the stretcher, looking at Isabel.

Quickly she said, "It's all gone now except in the shady places." She could have gnawed off her tongue. Now, of course, he would want the men to carry him around the north side of the house and show him those last patches.

"Papa!" she said, even while he was pointing. "Lay back and hush! Let's get you inside. You'll catch your death of cold."

She ran ahead of the bearers onto the porch, held open the door. Her eyes felt cold in her head, like silver spoons. She could have cried. Turning away, she looked down the hall where they would carry him, through a doorway to the old bed which filled the room like an abandoned river barge, washed up askew and catty-cornered. The counterpane was turned back, the pillow as white as a square of snow below the eaves, or somebody's flat grave marker.

The two men maneuvered the stretcher past, grazing her waist.

"That room straight ahead," Isabel said, standing thin against the wall. The men did not like her. She could tell that.

Then they carried him beyond her, toward the bed where he had jerked with joy when he fathered her, the same bed in which she had been wetly born, and Jasper, too. Twice her father had stood and looked down into that bed at what would survive him, and half the time he'd been wrong. Now he had a month or two of dying to do in that mammoth bed. After that, Isabel thought, she might burn the thing. Might leave it burning in the back field, below the old orchard. Might fly through the smoke of it, headed north, and not even look out the airplane window. She pressed her pocketbook where the stretcher had touched her, and followed them down the hall. Brenda can help burn it. Brenda wouldn't let me go through that funeral all alone. I doubt I can carry the bed outside by myself.

They laid him down and drew the sheets to his chin. Isabel signed the slip which said Marvin Perkins had been delivered with due care by the county ambulance service. On the way out, the short man pulled a small jar of pear preserves from his hip pocket. "Mama sent it," he said, and thrust it toward Isabel's front. "She's in his church. She said he liked pear preserves."

Isabel caught the jar against her purse. She'd forgotten what Papa liked and didn't like in the years she had been gone. Between now and Easter, she could not learn it all again. She was more grateful for the information than the fruit. She wanted to smile at the man, but she was a head taller and he kept his face down.

She held out her hand to the big one. "I believe you were in school with my brother."

"I played basketball with Jasper." The handshake was quick. "Got boys of my own playing now."

"That's fine," said Isabel, though really she thought it was depressing. "Thank you both."

Her father had gone instantly to sleep, the way a tired child will when at last he is dropped someplace familiar. Isabel stopped with her mouth open on the cheery word there was no need to say. On the pillow, his face even looked like a child's face, one which had been slightly crumpled. There were only a few wisps of hair on the pale scalp. Isabel laid his false teeth on the bedside table. He snuffled juicily in his sleep, like a baby or a bulldog. If she hurried, she could be back from the mailbox before he even wanted supper. She set the pear preserves beside the teeth.

The telephone rang in the hall.

It was Papa's preacher. She craned to see the clock. "Yes, he's asleep right now." Isabel felt through both pockets of her corduroy coat but could find no cigarettes. The preacher said something about food left on the kitchen table. By the churchwomen. Isabel said that was very nice. She braced the telephone on her shoulder and poured out her pocketbook and found cigarettes but no matches. "You'll tell them how much we appreciate it? Since I don't know the names? . . . Oh. Yes. Certainly."

Isabel made an ugly face at the framed picture of "Washington Crossing the Delaware" on the opposite wall. George, the boat, the tumbling waves: all painted in snuff, tar, nicotine. There was a pencil in the clutter from her bag and she wrote on the telephone book names the preacher spelled for her. With the eraser she poked Brenda's postcard into view. Cypress Gardens, for Christ's sake. "Yes." She thanked him again.

In the kitchen she found chicken broth and potato salad, two loaves of yeast bread, jars of beets and spiced apples, a bowl of ambrosia, a tall coconut cake on a cut-glass pedestal. They can't mean all that for a man who has cancer of the stomach, she thought. Most of that is for *me*. Deep in her throat there rose something smooth and solid, like a hard-boiled egg. They must have seen the coffee cups stacked in the sink, maybe even smelled the sticky glasses. What do I care if they poked through the kitchen? At home, Brenda won't even let me make toast.

Isabel poured the broth into a small pan, set it on the front burner of the stove, and looked at it. Globes of fat skated on the surface as if they were alive. Pushing the other food to one end of the table, she took her stationery box from a chair seat. There was a pack of matches inside with her pen. She wondered if the Baptist women had opened her stationery box and read the letter which still lay inside, face-down. She took out the two sheets and, lighting a cigarette and clicking her pen, read what she had written.

Dear Brenda,

Here I am in this ghastly hospital; I wish you could see it. No matter what waiting room I pick, somebody always sits beside me with a running sore, a bloody bandage, or a scar on his face where the skin was burned and snatched off. They don't get sick here, they get hurt. Axes and car jacks and hunting accidents. Even Papa still thinks it was carrying hay bales and feed that gave him his cancer. First he got hernia and then the hernia got mean.

But today they're sending Papa home and I have to

feed and nurse him to death. I do believe in mercy killing, I do. How could you watch this day after day and not believe in it? But if I had that power I don't know where I would stop. Two perfectly healthy boys have just walked through smelling of beer and motor oil, and I could poison them both.

I can't tell yet when I can come home. You can't imagine how far away from you I feel. This is some other planet. Papa's preacher is in and out, talking in whatever his language is—it can't be English. I never liked it here and it's worse now, at my age, when I've been living my own life so long. Nights I've been leaving the hospital to sleep in that house I never wanted to live in anymore. It's cold and empty. Everything you do in it makes a loud noise and everything Papa owns is made of tin and falls down in the night.

Nothing here is comfortable to me, and I don't mean the old plumbing or the mattresses that have fallen in. Even the parts of the house I thought I liked aren't there anymore. Four of us lived here and two are dead and one is dying, and it makes me nervous. The people who used this furniture don't use it anymore.

Isabel pinched off a piece of the cake icing and pushed it back in that space on her gum where a wisdom tooth should be. She drew a line across the page, deliberately sloping it upward in case Brenda should be looking for clues about her mood. Then she began to add in a firm, angular hand:

That reminds me of what I wanted to tell you about the bed.

She put out her cigarette. No point in pressing on with this letter when, even now, a long one from Brenda might lie in the mailbox. She buttoned her coat, hurried out the back door. As soon as she had gone halfway, Isabel began to fear Papa was calling, or the chicken broth had boiled all over the stove. She tried to run, mud spattering on her broad shoes and freckling her ankles. I must look like a grizzly bear, she thought, aching. The mailbox was empty.

She took her time walking back. Let him call. He'd be calling in an empty house if she was home in Baltimore where she belonged. Her shoes were such a mess she unlaced them at the back steps and left them there. The broth still waited over an unlit burner on the gas range. Isabel took off her coat. She ate a tablespoon of ambrosia. The linoleum was cold on her bare feet.

It was too soon to tell Brenda about the bed, how they could burn it together in the back field. At night. With Isabel pointing out the constellations. Save that for a surprise. Brenda would say, "What makes you think of such things!" And Brenda would giggle, carrying the slats out just the way Isabel said, and backing downstairs with her end of the stained old mattress.

Isabel sat down again to her letter. "That reminds me of what I wanted to tell you about the bed." She wrote:

Now we're at home and Papa's asleep in his big bed. I've moved it at an angle because the footboard is too tall to see over. God knows what makes Papa so cheerful, even about the snow he couldn't really see from the hospital. He's happy to have me here and says daughters will always come home when you need them. You know what a lie that is. But I want you to see this bed. It's a hundred years old, maybe two, and somebody built it out of trees cut down on the farm. It's put together with wooden pegs and they made it to last forever.

She got up and put some more ambrosia into a bowl and spooned it between sentences. There was a little sherry stirred into the juice.

Brenda, I wish you'd write more often. I need your letters. I don't see why you're going to the movies with Katherine Moose even if she is lonesome and has trouble getting her support checks. When did you ever have anything in common with Katherine Moose? (Which I mean as a compliment to you.) I thought you were going to make a decoupage table while I was gone, for the living room? After this house, I'll be glad to see something colorful. All Mama ever hung on these walls was that fellow hoeing in the fields, the Horse Fair, cathedrals, that St. Bernard in the woods with the children, George Washington, and Gainsborough's Blue Boy. All of them, even the blue boy, painted in brown gravy. I am so depressed. . . .

Papa was calling. Isabel flicked on the gas under his broth and hurried to the bedroom.

"Who's that?" he cried when she came in. More and more, Isabel thought, he comes out of sleep into a world he's half forgotten. Maybe the world was for him like this house to Isabel. Not even the good parts looking like they used to.

"It's Isabel," she said, as gently as she could. She knew her voice was too loud for a sickroom. The nurses had said so. Even the doctor whispered, while touching her father with rapid, hairy hands.

"Isabel? That you?"

"You're home." She eased to his side and laid one hand on his arm, to show she was real. If he asks about Jasper, I don't know what I'll say.

"You've got things fixed up real nice. Even the cobwebs swept down. You've not been washing this old woodwork?" He struggled higher on the pillow. Isabel shook her head. "It looks whiter. What time is it?"

"I'll bring you some soup. You never saw so much food. Mrs. . . . Mrs. Bradford. And two others. And somebody sent you pear preserves." She nudged the jar but he reached beyond it for his teeth in their gauze wrapping. "I'll get your supper now. You need anything first? You need the bedpan?" Isabel didn't know why she asked, since by now she knew he was like any other animal and did not defecate until after a meal. She and Brenda had an Airedale at home the same way. "You get your teeth in," she said, although he was already settling his jaws with a few bites of empty air.

She arranged his tray carefully by the bed, then sat in a chair where the high footboard hid him. She did not like to watch him eat. Tonight she looked at the room itself, improved somehow just because it had Papa to belong to. The wide floorboards had mellowed from years of traffic. Two braided rugs were faded gray. Under the bed the lint curled back, and softly under Mama's treadle sewing machine, behind her domed tin trunk stamped with flowers, then under the bureau with its three-foot mirror.

The mirror was in such a condition nobody was safe looking into it. Its surface had peeled and bubbled along jagged stripes of gold and gray. Isabel had glanced in it her first day home and discovered a face that, for all its broadness, looked frail and insane.

Neither she nor Papa could see themselves in the mirror now, after her struggle to move the furniture. Getting ready to bring him home, Isabel had lain in the big bed where he would lie, just to be certain. No need, she'd thought, for Papa to see how his skin had yellowed, his eyes shrunk away from their bony cups. Papa's fine black eyes lay now in their sockets like two butter beans. Isabel smiled. Brenda wouldn't know what a butter bean was. The Baptist women will bring some when Papa dies; Brenda can taste them then. She'll feel sorry for all I've had to bear these last weeks. She'll be sorry she didn't write more letters.

In front of the mirror on an embroidered spread was Papa's stopped cookie of a watch, two combs, shaving mug, brush. A china heart which held buttons, cuff links, and moldering tie-clasps. In the bottom corners of the leprous mirror two photographs were stuck: one of Isabel, age 10, riding a mule; and one of Jasper in his army uniform. She'd been tempted to put these in a drawer but decided she didn't have the right. From where Papa lay, they wouldn't look much larger than postage stamps.

Behind the high wall of his bed, Papa said, "How's it feel to be home? Not counting me sick and all?"

"Not the way I remember it," Isabel said. She was glad she could not see the way he siphoned up his soup.

"You never did come home much. You sure you can get off work this long?"

"I'm sure. I'm good at my job, you know."

"I hate costing you money. You was always tight about money, not like Jasper." The slurping stopped. He said, "And that's a good thing. Here you are, independent. No worries. Nobody telling you what to do. I'm that way myself."

He did not know how long ago his insurance money had been used up, couldn't guess how much Isabel had paid the hospital. With her cruise money. She and Brenda had meant to go to Greece this summer. She said, "Your preacher called, wants to come see you. I told him tomorrow morning. Get you over the trip. Get your strength up." She could not tell whether he laughed or choked.

Then at last came the question she had dreaded. "When's Jasper coming?" He had already asked it once, just after the operation.

"Papa," she said, but he was ahead of her.

"That's right, Jasper's dead. It's the fault of the medicine. With the medicine I can't tell what time it is."

Isabel said it was seven o'clock. "Soon be time for . . . well, not for bed. For sleep."

"I don't mean clocks," he said crossly, and the dishes rattled when he put the tray on the table. "They's not a thing wrong with my mind and don't you forget it. The medicine flattens things out, that's all. It can send you into any year it damn well pleases."

Isabel thought this was not a good time to remind him to take another dose. She cleared the dishes, slid the bedpan under his blanket, and went to the kitchen to put food away. She carried her cigarettes to the back steps, because when he was awake smoke made Papa cough, and coughing made Papa hurt. The mud had hardened on her shoes like concrete. When she put them on, the earth dragged at her soles. She clumped around the yard. I told Brenda it was like another planet here. Even gravity pulls harder.

She could barely see the mailbox in the growing dark. Tomorrow, at least, one of Brenda's damned postcards. Brenda taught third grade in a private school for Jewish children, and all year long she made them bring in postcards showing vacation spots in fifty states. Brenda would never have to buy a postcard in her entire life. Especially being so stingy with them. So far, Isabel had only received Natural Bridge, Virginia, and the Cypress Gardens, both with a hole where they had once been thumbtacked to a display board. Both said much the same.

> Busy at school. Had to get new battery your car. Hope things aren't too bad. Letter follows love Brenda. Can't write going to movie with Katherine but got your letter and will answer soon.

Isabel had jammed that one inside her pocketbook so hard the shiny surface folded and made a long crease up the Southern belle in her hoop skirt.

She flattened her cigarette with a weighted foot. When she padded in bedroom slippers to Papa's room, carrying the medicine bottle and spoon, he was already asleep and the bedpan waited for her on the table, as neatly covered with the napkin as a plate of cooling rolls. It won't be long, thought Isabel, before I'll be giving him a needle in his arm, the way the doctor showed me. "You've got a real knack for this," he had said when she plunged distilled water into the orange. "You'd have made a good nurse."

"I don't talk soft enough," Isabel had said.

She woke her father and made him take the medicine, though he swore he didn't need it tonight. They had an argument. In the end, she jammed the spoon into his mouth while he was still fussing, and made a small reddening dent on his upper gum. He pulled back, stiff, on the pillow and held the liquid in his mouth. His cheeks blew out like a squirrel's.

"You swallow that now," she said. He would not.

"I didn't mean to hurt you. Please swallow it down."

Still he lay rigid, his eyes black, neck hard, chin sharp.

She said, "Jasper would want you to take the medicine." Her father closed his eyes. The bulb jerked in his throat. His face relaxed. Isabel laid her hand on his forehead, but he would not move and he was not going to open his eyes. "Good night, Papa," she said, trying to make her voice soft, and thinking, God-damn him, damn Jasper, damn Brenda, damn them all.

Jasper's bedroom was the most comfortable place in the old farmhouse and that was the only reason Isabel was sleeping there. A late addition, the room had electrical outlets in the baseboards and less bulky, gloomy furnishings. Jasper's old books still lined the shelves he and Papa had built, and she and Jasper had painted.

A broad map of Korea was tacked on one wall, a green peninsula touching the Sea of Japan, Manchuria, and the Yellow Sea. A snaky line of black crayon marked the places Jasper might have been, battles in which he might have fought. Papa had kept this record against the day Jasper came home to tell them everything. Near Wonju, the black line broke off. Once Jasper died, in February, 1951, the whole Eighth Army, the war itself, stopped dead and hung uncompleted on Jasper's wall.

Isabel looked at the fading map while she put on pajamas. She plugged in Jasper's reading lamp and ran one finger along his books. *Tom Swift.* Zane Grey. *Tarzan and the Jewels of Opar. Kidnapped. Wuthering Heights. Boy Scout Handbook.* Dog and horse stories. True stories of the F.B.I. *Tobacco Road. Dutchess Hotspur.* Frank Harris.

From the flyleaf of *Robin Hood,* she read the blurred lines scrawled across the treetops of Sherwood Forest:

> *You steal my book*
> *And I can tell*
> *You'll go to Hell.*
> *Marvin Jasper Perkins, Jr. Age 9½*

Sometimes on the map of her own mind Isabel tried to draw the rest of Jasper's life—to crayon him home across the Pacific, over the continent to Carolina, to some good Northern college on the G.I. Bill and what money Isabel would have given him. What was a cruise to Greece compared to that investment?

And now Jasper would be . . . forty-one years old, two more than Isabel was now. And they might be sitting here tonight, in Papa's house, waiting out Papa's death together.

She had always been larger than Jasper. By now he, too, would have added weight. Maybe his pale hair would have thinned, the capillaries begun to surface in his cheeks. Her income would have been higher than his—and how Jasper would have hated that! He'd have told her for the hundredth time to let her hair grow long. Isabel took a bottle of Scotch and a glass from a drawer. They could have shared a drink, talked about things. About Brenda. About whoever Jasper might have had to talk about.

Papa called out. Isabel put her drink behind the photograph of Jasper in his high-school mortarboard. She went to the back bedroom, but he was asleep again from the medicine that could send him into any year it pleased.

"I'm still here, Papa," she said, just in case he could hear. Then she went to bed.

. . . Jasper moves swiftly ahead of me through the thick forest. Sometimes he swings from vines; at others, he is simply thrown lightly from one great tree to another. I am riding more slowly behind him on the ground, on the back of something shaped like a mule but much larger. Nearly the size of an elephant. I am happy, but I wish he would wait for me. We are going to a cleared space he knows, to build our house. He calls down to me that the Indians are coming. He calls down that we will need help in building our house. I am to choose some Indian to help us. Now I see the line of natives marching, a column in single file. All are women, very dark brown, young, healthy, as tall as the animal which carries me. They wear nothing but short skirts made of black feathers. I pick a girl I think Jasper will like. She looks very strong. Now I see another who resembles her; she says the two of them are sisters. Perhaps they are even twins. I decide to choose both girls to help us in the clearing where Jasper is waiting for me. . . .

When Isabel woke, the thick forest turned into a network of tree-branch shadows thrown by the morning sun on the walls and floor and across the four-legged bed. Her mouth was dry. Her head ached and seemed to be full of fungus. She got up, feeling tired, and put the Scotch back inside Jasper's bureau. She decided to wear her wool slacks because the preacher probably wouldn't like slacks.

She made Papa's oatmeal and soft-boiled egg and woke him. He looked into her face as if he had never seen it before.

She said it twice. "Time for breakfast."

His eyes slowly remembered what breakfast was. She put

another pillow behind his head and shoulders. "Want you to eat early and get cleaned up. Your preacher's coming."

"Good morning, Isabel," he finally said. In a minute he smiled.

He ate as if he were really hungry. It depressed her to think of all that good food, falling down into that internal ruin. "You're not a bad cook, Isabel," he said, not noticing, as she did, the oatmeal spilling onto the sheets. "For somebody that always hated cooking. You fix your own meals in Baltimore?"

"Anybody can make oatmeal." She stored his empty suitcase in the closet, under the suit he would likely be buried in. "Maybe we'll have time to change those sheets."

"You should of got married," Papa said.

"I'm better off than plenty married people. Tomorrow you want a poached egg?"

"I never could stand an egg looked like it had just fell out of the nest. You really don't miss it? Your friends married and all?"

"My friends aren't married."

"You're not old yet. Maybe you're courting? You and your roommate go out much? You and Sheila?"

Isabel gave him the yellow capsule. "I haven't lived with Sheila for over a year now. Sheila turned out to be somebody I couldn't respect. I don't even see her anymore. Want some more water?"

"What are you getting so mad for? You and the new one, then. You find any bachelors to take you to supper?"

"Brenda. Her name is Brenda." She decided to brush the sheets off and leave them. Why make the preacher think a dying man was neat? "Anything else?"

"Open the window," Papa said. "Maybe it's started to smell like spring."

Isabel took the preacher to Papa's bedroom, waited

politely while they talked about Easter, baseball, plans for the new church—none of which Marvin Perkins would live to see. She had never met so tactless a man as that preacher, and she stood behind the high footboard and made disapproving faces until even her scalp was tired. He kept right on telling Papa what a fine time the youth club would have camping by the river when it got warm, and how they'd moved the revival to August.

At last he began to read Scripture—which was all he was supposed to do in the first place, thought Isabel. He started the Sermon on the Mount, but Papa said he'd like something older than that, something sterner.

"I've got to like the Old Testament again," he said, sounding embarrassed, as if this were a breach of taste. "What I really like is the wars against the Philistines."

"I see." The preacher began leafing back.

"After Moses, though," said Papa. He settled back and spread his arms wide on the counterpane, palms up. Like a horizontal shrug. "I never thought it was right Moses got shut out of the Promised Land."

That would have tickled Brenda! The preacher began to read about armies, battles, the fear of the Lord. Isabel excused herself, took down her coat from its peg in the hall, and went into the yard, knocking clay off her shoes. The jonquils were already up, their buds like cartridges. There were red knots on the twigs of the maple she and Jasper had climbed. Jasper once climbed to the very top of that tree because it had been his ambition to spit down the house chimney; and he did, but he missed.

Through Papa's half-open window she could hear that the story was about Moab, the Canaanites, and Deborah the prophetess: ". . . for the Lord shall sell Sisera into the hand of a woman," the preacher read.

Isabel circled to the backyard. Here the orchard spread downhill to the back field, bottomland, a winding creek. There were broken limbs still caught in the fruit trees, jelly-filled wounds in trunks where peach borers waited out the winter. Last year's caterpillar webs flapped on the cherries like wet old flags.

"You've quit tending the orchard?" She'd asked Papa that in the hospital, on some choking, long, steam-heated after-noon.

"Not much point after your mama died. Too much to eat raw, and nobody to make jam or cobbler." Talk of the orchard revived him, though he was very weak from surgery. "I never liked sprays and poisons. Used to go out and kill everything by hand. That way, a worm knew who it was and I knew who I was." His cheeks grew red as apples. At that time, the doctor was saying he would live either a day or two months, depend-ing on which his heart decided and how fast his stomach ate itself. "It still blooms, though, down that whole hillside. Not as much fruit, but how it does bloom!"

Now she paced downhill, wondering if he would wait to see it blossom one more time, ducking her head under the limbs of the Bartlett pear. Bartlett was self-sterile; she'd heard him say you needed another variety to cross-pollinate. He'd set another pear far down the hill. Isabel looked for it, but all the bare trees looked alike at a distance.

When Papa's done with the bed, I'll burn it there. In the bottomland. Primitive ritual, I'll tell Brenda. Like putting a Viking to sea on his flaming barge. It'll be just pagan enough to suit an anti-Semite Jewess like Brenda. She'll shiver while she's laughing. "Isabel, there's nobody like you in the world!" she'll say. But she'll be uneasy about it, too, and we'll need a drink when we get back inside, in Jasper's room.

Then Isabel thought one more step: she saw herself home and telling the other women in their apartment building. Katherine Moose. And Rhonda. She imagined how easy it would be to boast, to repeat when she was drunk and maudlin. "So the country Baptists got the body to bury, but the real ceremony was mine. Father and offspring, just like that." Offspring. I could make a pun on bedspring if I was sober. And Brenda would echo the telling in mock horror. "I said, Isabel, you can't do that! But you know Isabel, she'd been down there till she needed to be *cauterized,* or something, so I took one end and . . ."

In the distance, Isabel heard the preacher's car. Hurrying to the house, she forgot to bend her head and some tree—the pear?—raked a limb through her short hair.

There was still no letter and that night Isabel tried to call Brenda Goldstein. The telephone in their Baltimore apartment was first busy, and later unanswered. She tried the number several times. When she finally got through at eleven-thirty, there seemed to be a party going on.

"Brenda? It's Isabel. What in the world is all that noise?"

"Turn that thing down. Hello?"

"I said it's Isabel! I've been calling for hours."

"I went to an art lecture. What's the matter? Has he died?"

Isabel was angry and said, too loud, "NO, HE HAS NOT DIED!" She wondered if Papa could have heard. "He's about the same. I just wanted to talk to you. I haven't had a letter for two weeks."

"Well, I mailed you one." A crowd was milling around that apartment, talking, laughing, shaking ice cubes.

"Listen, it gets lonesome down here." Isabel decided she must speak softer, much softer. She stared at George Washington, who seemed to her afloat in rapids of Scotch and seltzer. She eyed the canal in Venice on the other wall, painted in shades of bourbon whiskey thinned down with spit. "Listen," she hissed, "where were you all night long with me calling and calling?"

"I told you. I went with Katherine Moose to an art lecture."

Isabel said it sounded like they were having a goddamn party.

"Well, Ron's here from next door. And Sheila. We ran into Sheila at the museum."

Isabel paced up and down on the gleaming heart-pine boards. "It's all right for Rhonda to be there, but you know, Brenda, you *know* Sheila's not to set foot in that apartment! Brenda, you know that! As many times as I've said . . ."

"Yes," came a stiff, polite voice. "It was a *very* good lecture. Manet."

"Oh, Christ," said Isabel. "And Sheila just can't wait to see what changes you've made in the apartment. Rode her home in my car, I'll bet! I can imagine. She can't wait to tell you all my faults while I'm down here keeping a deathwatch. You hear me, Brenda? A deathwatch! I never thought the minute my back was turned . . ."

"Well, you try to get some sleep and not break your own health over it," Brenda said, and hung up.

Isabel couldn't sleep at all. She rolled from one edge of Jasper's bed to the other. She was almost grateful when Papa cried out with pain in the night, but the hurt was gone before she got to him. He was sleeping. The gray folds of skin under his neck hung loose. He breathed in and out, in and out.

I meant to offer him those pear preserves for supper,

thought Isabel. I'd have thought of it if Brenda had stayed home where she belonged, and my mind had been easy. In and out he breathed. She moved her arm toward his tall mirror where reflected light showed up her wristwatch. Three-thirty. Isabel wound the watch. She did not look at her image.

She went into the hall and dialed, direct, the number of their apartment. Out of a dry and swollen mouth, Brenda said, "Hello?"

Isabel said nothing.

"Hello? Who is this?"

Isabel breathed heavily into the telephone. In and out. In and OUT.

"What number are you calling?" said Brenda.

(She's sitting up in bed now and reaching for her robe. She covers up with that fluffy robe even to talk on the phone. Her throat's probably scratching. In the morning her head will ache right over both mastoid bones. Oh, I know her. She'll look older than thirty-five in the morning, and there'll be lines on her face where the pillowcase wrinkled. . . .)

Shaking with the laugh she was holding back, Isabel blew two hard puffs of air into the mouthpiece.

Then she heard a second voice, a woman's voice, say, ". . . answers, just hang up."

There was a single click, then the long singing as emptiness rushed along the black highway, beside the asphalt road, by the rutted road, down the wires to Isabel, across the state of Virginia, humming inland over the muddy yard, into the house and through her ear and into her brain, like that old tent peg the Hebrew woman nailed through the brain of Sisera when he took refuge in her tent.

Still Life
with Fruit

≠

Although Gwen said three times she felt fine, the sister made her sit in a wheelchair and be rolled to the elevator like some invalid. Looking over her shoulder for Richard, she let one hand drop onto the rubber tire, which scraped heat into her fingertips. Immediately Gwen repeated on the other side, for her fingers felt clammy and disconnected from the rest of her.

"Your husband can't come up for a while, dear," said the sister, parking her neatly in one corner and pressing the Number 4 button. Sister was broad in the hip and wore a white skirt starched stiff as poster paper. "Are the pains bad?"

"No." Gwen sat rigid and cold, all the blood gone to her fingers. There was so much baby jammed toward her lungs that lifting her chest would have been ridiculous. Surely the sister knew enough to say "contraction," and never "pain." For some women—not Gwen, of course—that could be a serious psychological mistake.

Besides, they weren't bad. Maybe not bad enough. Gwen had no fear of childbirth, since she understood its stages perfectly, but to make a fool of herself with false labor? She'd never bear the embarrassment. To so misread the body's deepest messages—that would be like wetting one's pants onstage.

She said uneasily, "I hope they're not slowing down."

The sister's face grew briefly alert, perhaps suspicious. "When's your due date?"

Gwen told her ten days ago, and the sister said, "That's all right, then." Maybe if Gwen were Catholic, the sister's face would seem kinder, even blessed. That led to the idea— quickly pushed aside—that had she been Catholic, bearing the first in a long row of unimpeded babies, the sister would like her better.

On Ward 4 she was rolled to a special room, told to put on the backless nightshirt and get into bed.

"And drink water. Drink lots of water," the sister said, took her blood pressure, and left her with a thermometer cocked at an angle in her mouth.

Gwen couldn't recall anything in the doctor's pamphlets about drinking water. Maybe in this hospital it was sanctified? She jerked both hands to her abdomen, relieved when it tightened and hardened the way Dr. Somers had been promising for months. She hoped this new pang was on schedule; Richard's watch was still on Richard's arm, downstairs. She felt no pain, since she was a well-adjusted modern who accepted her womanhood. Two months ago, however, she'd decided not to try natural childbirth, mainly because the doctor who advocated it was male. She was drifting then away from everything male. Lately she had withdrawn from everything, period. (The baby has eaten me, she sometimes thought.)

She climbed into the high bed, suddenly angry and alone, and discovered on the wall facing her a bronze statuette of

Jesus wrenched on His cross, each shoulder drawn in its joint, His neck roped from pain, His face turned out with agony. It struck Gwen that Catholics might be downright insensitive. The Virgin Mary was one thing, but in this room on this day, this prince . . . this chaste bachelor on his way to God's bosom? To Gwen it seemed . . . well . . . tasteless.

Another sister recorded her 98.6 temperature and drew an assortment of blood samples on glass slides and in phials. She sucked these up through a flexible brown tube and Gwen wondered if she ever sipped too hard and got a mouthful. The sister also wrote down what Mrs. Gower had eaten and how recently, and made her urinate into a steel bowl. "You take a nap, till the barber comes," she said. And giggled.

But Gwen, crackling with energy, doubled her pillow behind her and sat nearly upright, wide eyes fixed on the wracked form of Jesus in a loincloth. They must have already cast lots for His seamless robe (down on the cool, gray hospital tile) but at this stage in the crucifixion no one had yet buried a spear point in His side. He was skinnier than Gwen had always pictured Him.

Ah, to be skinny herself! To sleep on her flat stomach, walk lightly again on the balls of her feet. To own a navel that would be a hole and not a hill! Gwen made herself bear down once, as if on the toilet. No effect at all. Too early.

The labor room, pale green, was furnished in buffed aluminum. Its single chair was dull metal, straight, uncomfortable. Her clothes had been hung in a green wall locker next to Jesus, including the linen dress with the 24-inch waist she hoped to wear home next week. On her bedside table was a pitcher of water and crushed ice, and a glass with a clear tube in it. She drank water as the sister had ordered. Maybe it wet down the sliding ramp where Junior, like some battleship, would be launched to the open sea. He felt to her like a battleship, plated turrets and stacks and projections, each pricking her own organs until they withdrew and gave him room. She sometimes felt as if her lungs had slipped slightly into each arm and her entrails been driven down her thighs.

The next nurse wore black religious garb, its hem nearly to the floor. With a black arm she set her covered tray on Gwen's mattress, said it was time for the first shave in Mrs. Gower's life, and flicked off the sheet. Gwen pressed into the pillow. She had never felt so naked—even after months of probes with gloved fingers and cold entries of the doctor's periscope. It must be a sign of her failing brain that one minute she saw her baby as a battleship; now there were periscopes thrust up his launching ramp. She had not thought clearly since that first sperm hit the egg and blew fuses all the way upstairs. Even her paintings showed it. Haphazard smears on canvas, with no design at all. Richard pretended, still, to admire them. He pretended the thought never crossed his mind that she might slice off one ear. She might have, too, if she could remember where the thing was growing.

It was the stare of a woman which embarrassed her. A religious. The young sister gazed with interest between Gwen's thighs as she made ready to repeat (here Gwen giggled) what Delilah did to Samson. She thought of asking the nun whether work in a maternity ward lent new appeal to chastity.

The nun said brightly, "Here we are."

"Here *we* are?" Gwen laughed again. I'm getting giddy. There must be dope in that water pitcher.

"You're very hairy." The sister couldn't be over twenty years old. Perhaps she was still apprenticed, a novice. Sleeping single in her narrow bed, spending her days with women who slept double and who now brought her the ripe fruits of

God. Her face looked pure and pale, as if she were preparing to cross herself in some holy place. So it was a shock when she said, "All beautiful women are hairy. We had a movie star here once, miscarried on a promotion tour, and you could have combed her into ringlets."

Gwen could not match that, so she lay, eyes closed, while the dull razor yanked out her pubic essence by the roots. She could no longer remember how she would look there, bald. She could recall sprouting her first scattered hairs as a girl, each lying flat and separate. Sparse, very soft in texture. Now would she grow back prickly? Now, when she most needed to recapture Richard, would she scrape him like a cheese grater? Five o'clock shadow in the midnight place? When Gwen opened her eyes, it seemed to her Jesus had been nailed at just the right height to get a good view from His cross.

At last the sister's pan was black with sheep shearings. Black sheep, have you any wool? One for the unborn boy, who lives up the lane? Gwen drank more water while the sister took out the razor blade and wiped the last hairs on a cloth.

"When can my husband come?" asked Gwen. She felt her face pucker. "I don't have anything to read."

The sister smiled. "Maybe after the enema." She carried out her woolly pan. Maybe she stuffed sofa cushions. And the bloodletting nun reclined on them and sipped Type O cocktails through her soft rubber tube. Maybe a "hair shirt" really meant . . .

Why, I'm just furious! Gwen thought, surprised. I'm almost homicidal!

The nurse with the enema must have been poised outside the door. Gwen barely had time to test her shaved skin with shocked fingers. Plucked chicken butt. She ought to keep her fingers away—germs. Had she not just lately picked her own nose? Maybe she bore some deep, subconscious hostility against her baby!

She jerked her hand away and lifted her hips, as she was told, onto the rubber sheet. She refused to hear the cheery conversation floating between her knees. Inside her the liquid burned. When she belched, she feared the enema had risen all the way. She might sneeze and twin spurts jet out her ears. She gasped, "I can't—can't hold it in."

Quickly she was helped across the room to the toilet cubicle. God, she would never make it. She carried herself, a brimming bowl, with the least possible movement. Then she could let go and spew full every sewer pipe in the whole hospital. Through the plastic curtain the nun said happily, "You doing just fine, Mrs. Gower?" Now *there* was psychology!

"O.K.," she managed to say. "Can my husband come now?"

"You just sit there awhile," said the nun, and carried her equipment to the next plucked chicken down the hall.

Disgusting how clean the bathroom was. Gwen was a bad housekeeper—as Richard's parents kept hinting—but she couldn't see why. She was always at work, twenty projects under way at once; yet while she emptied the wastebasket, soap crud caked in the soap dish and flecks of toothpaste flew from nowhere onto the mirror. Nor could she keep pace with Richard's bladder. The disinfectant was hardly dry before he peed again and splattered everything. Yet, enemas and all, this place was clean as a monk's or a nun's cell.

Gwen flushed the toilet but did not stand. In case. She never felt so alone. Ever since she crossed two states to live in a house clotted with Gowers, she had been shrinking. The baby ate her. Now the baby's container was huge but Gwen, invisible, had no body to live in. Today she had been carried to the hospital like a package. This end up. Open with care.

"Ready for bed?"

She cleaned herself one more time and tottered out. The new nurse was in plain uniform, perhaps even agnostic. She set a cheap clock by the water pitcher. "How far apart are your pains now?"

Gwen had forgotten them. "I don't know." She was sleepy.

"Have you had any show?"

Gwen couldn't remember what "show" was. Some plug? Mucus. She didn't know. Was she expected to know everything? Couldn't the fool nurse look on the sheets and tell? She was probably Catholic, too, and her suit was in the cleaners.

"Your husband can visit a minute now. And your doctor's on the floor."

Gwen fell back on the skimpy pillow. She drowsed, one hand dropped like a fig-leaf over her cool pubis.

"How's it going?" Richard said. His voice was very loud.

"Going!" Gwen flew awake. "It's gone!" she said bitterly. "Gone down the toilet! I don't even have any phlegm left in my throat. All of it. Whoosh." Suddenly he looked a good five years younger than she, tanned, handsome. Joe College. He looked well fed, padded with meat and vegetables, plump with his own cozy waste from meat and vegetables. "Where in hell have you been?"

"In the waiting room." He yanked his smile into a straight line. "You having a bad time?"

She stared at the ceiling. "They shaved me."

"Oh." He gave a laugh nearly dry enough for a sympathetic cluck. Give the little chicken a great big cluck. Ever since they'd moved in with his parents, Gwen had been the Outsider and Richard the Hypocrite. If she talked liberal and Mr. Gower conservative, Richard said nervously they shared the same goals. When he left mornings for work, he kissed her good-bye in the bedroom and his mother in the kitchen. If Gwen fixed congealed salad and Mother Gower made tossed fruit, Richard ate heartily of both and gave equal praise. Lately Gwen had been drawing his caricature, in long black strokes, and he thought it was Janus.

He said, "I never thought about shaving, but it must be necessary. The doctor can probably see things better."

Things? Gwen turned her face away. Cruelly she said, "It's probably easier to clean off the blood."

"Hey, Gwen," he said, and bent to kiss as much cheek as he could reach. She grabbed him. So hard it must have pinched his neck. Poor little man with a pinch on his neck! She stuck her tongue deep in his mouth and then bit his lower lip.

Uneasy, he sat in the metal chair and held her hand. "Whatever they're giving you, let's take some home," he said.

And go through this again? At first, in their rented room, she and Richard had lain in bed all day on Sundays. Sleeping and screwing, and screwing and sleeping. My come got lost in the baby's Coming. I don't even remember how it feels.

But Dr. Somers, when he came in, looked to Gwen for the first time virile and attractive. A little old, but he'd never be clumsy. For medical reasons alone, he'd never roll sleepily away and leave her crammed against the wall with a pillow still under her ass, swollen and hot. With Richard's parents on the other side of that wall, breathing lightly and listening.

She gave Dr. Somers a whore's smile to show him her hand lay in Richard's with no more feeling than paper in an envelope.

"You look just fine, Gwendolyn," he said. He nodded to

Richard as if he could hardly believe a young squirt with no obvious merits could have put her in such a predicament. "We'll take a look now and see how far along things are. Mr. Gower?"

Richard went into the hall. She watched Dr. Somers put ooze on his rubber glove. Talking with him down the valley of uplifted knees seemed now more normal than over the supper table to Richard. She had lost her embarrassment with him. Besides, Dr. Somers liked art. He continued to talk to her as if the baby had not yet eaten her painting hand, her eye for line and color. As if there would still be something of Gwen left when this was over.

While he fumbled around in her dampness, he often asked what she was painting now, or raved about Kandinsky. When she first went to his office with two missed menstrual periods, she mentioned the prints hung in his waiting room. "Black Lines" was Dr. Somers's favorite—he had seen the original at the Guggenheim on a convention in New York.

Gwen had not told him when, in her sixth month, her own admiration settled instead on Ivan Albright. Her taste shifted to Albright's warty, funereal textures, even while her disconnected hand continued to play with a palette knife and lampblack dribble. The few times her brain could get hold of the proper circuits, it made that hand pour together blobs of Elmer's glue, lighter fluid, and India ink. *Voilà!* Mitosis extended! She had also done a few charcoal sketches of herself nude and pregnant, with no face at all under the wild black hair, or with a face rounded to a single, staring eye.

Oh, she was sore where he slid his finger! Politely he nodded uphill toward her head. "Glaswell has a sculpture in the lobby, did you see it?"

"We came in the other door."

"I was on the purchasing committee. It's metal and fiber-glass, everything straining upward. That answered the board's request for a modern work consistent with the Christian view of man." He frowned. "You're hardly dilated at all. When did you feel the last one?"

"I stopped feeling anything right after that enema."

He thrust deeper. "False alarm, I'm afraid. But your departure date—when is it? I want you well rested before a long trip."

"In two weeks." Richard was being drafted. Once he left for the army, Gwen would take the baby home to her parents. The Gowers expected her to stay here, of course, but she would not. Last week she had given Dr. Somers all her good reasons, one by one. When the baby came, she planned to give them to Richard. And if he dared balk, she intended to go into a post-partum depression which would be a medical classic.

He laughed. "The baby's not following your schedule." His round head shook, and behind his thick glasses his eyes floated like ripe olives. "It's a false alarm, all right."

"But it happened just the way you said. An ache in the back. That cramp feeling. And it settled down right by the clock." To her humiliation, Gwen started to cry. "I'm overdue, goddamn it. He must weigh fifty pounds up there. What in hell is he waiting for?"

Dr. Somers withdrew and stripped off the glove. He looked at Jesus thoughtfully. He scrubbed his hands in a steel pan. "Tell you what, Gwendolyn. Stop that crying now. It's supper-time anyway; let's keep you overnight. A little castor oil at bedtime. If nothing happens by morning, I'll induce labor."

"You can skip the castor oil," Gwen said, sniffing hard. "It'll go through me like . . . like a marble down a drainpipe." She did not know how he might induce labor. Some powerful uterine drug? She pictured herself convulsing, held down by a crowd of orderlies and priests. "Induce it how?"

"Puncture the membranes," he said cheerfully. He looked so merry she got an ugly superimposed picture: boy, straight pin, balloons. "I'll just have a word with your husband."

An hour later, they demoted Gwen from the labor room and down the hall to a plain one, where she lay alongside a woman who was pleased to announce she had just had her tubes tied. "And these old Roman biddies hate it. Anybody that screws ought to get caught at it—that's their motto."

The Roman biddy who happened to be helping Gwen into bed did not even turn, although her face blotched an uneven red. Her cheeks ripened their anger as disconnected from her soul, as Gwen's painting hand was adrift from her brain. Among the red patches, the biddy's mouth said, perfectly controlled, "I wouldn't talk too much, Mrs. Gower. I'd get my rest."

The woman in the next bed was Ramona Plumpton, and she had four babies already. With this last one she'd nearly bled to death. "This is the best hospital in town, though, and I'm a Baptist. The food's good and it's the cleanest. No staph infections." Behind one hand she added, "I hear, though, they'll save the baby first, no matter what. That puts it down to a fifty-fifty chance in my book. Is this your first, honey?"

"Yes. They're going to induce labor so I can travel soon. My husband's joining the army." She hoped Richard would not mention false labor, not in front of this veteran.

"You're smart to follow him from camp to camp." Perhaps to counteract her hemorrhage, Mrs. Plumpton had painted rosy apples on each cheek. "The women that hang around after soldiers! You wouldn't believe it!"

Gwen thought about that. There she'd be, home with her

beard growing out, while Richard entered some curly, practiced woman. Huge breasts with nipples lined like a pair of
prunes. Like Titian, she arranged the woman, adjusted the
light. She made the woman cock one heavy arm so she could
stipple reddish fur underneath.

"Bringing it on like that, you'll birth fast," said Mrs. Plumpton. "A dry birth, but fast. I was in labor a day and a half with
my first and I've got stretch marks you wouldn't believe.
Calvin says I look like the tattooed lady."

Gwen assigned Mrs. Plumpton's broad, blushing face to
the prostitute in Fort Bragg and tied off her tubes with a scar-
let ribbon.

Richard came by but said he wasn't allowed to stay. He'd
driven all the way uptown to bring Gwen some books—one of
Klee prints and a *Playboy* magazine and three paperbacks
about British murders. Gwen usually enjoyed multiple murders behind the vicarage, after tea, discovered by spinsters
and solved by Scotland Yard.

He kissed her very tenderly and she stared into one of his
eyes. The large woman was imprinted there already, peach-
colored, her heart of gold glowing through her naked skin.

"It's very common and you're not to feel bad about it."

She touched Richard's mouth with her fingers. Did a dry
birth have anything in common with dry sex? It sounded
harder. She reached beyond him and drank a whole glass of
water.

". . . Dr. Somers says there's nothing to it. I'll be here
tomorrow long before anything happens."

"Now don't you worry," Gwen said, just to remind him
what his duty was. She got down a little more water.

Richard said his parents, downstairs, were not allowed to

visit. "They send you their love. Mom's getting everything ready."

Sweeping lint from under our marriage bed. Straightening my skirts on their hangers. She can't come near my cosmetics without tightening every lid and bottle cap.

"Mom's a little worried about induced labor. Says it doesn't seem natural." He patted her through the sheet. "They've both come to love you like a daughter."

When he had gone, Ramona Plumpton said, "Well, he's good-*looking*." It wasn't much, she meant, but it was something. "Between you and him, that ought to be a pretty baby. You want a boy or a girl?"

"Girl." They had mainly discussed a son, to bear both grandfathers' names. William Everest Gower. Suddenly she did want a daughter. And she'd tell her from the first that school dances, fraternity pins, parked cars—it all led down to this. This shaved bloat in a bed with a reamed-out gut.

She read until the nurse brought castor oil, viscous between two layers of orange juice. It made her gag, but she got it down.

For a long time she could not sleep. Too many carts of metal implements were rolled down the hall; plowshares rattled in buckets, and once a whole harvesting machine clashed out of the elevator.

When she finally drifted off, she dreamed she found her baby hanging on a wall. Its brain had grown through the skull like fungus, and suspended from its wafer head was a neckless wet sac with no limbs at all. Gwen started to cry and a priest came in carrying a delicate silver pitchfork. He told her to hush, he hadn't opened the membranes yet. When he pricked the soft bag, it fell open and spilled out three perfect male babies, each of them no bigger than her hand, and each with a rosebud penis tipped with one very tiny thorn. The priest began to circumcise them in the name of the Father, Son, and Holy Ghost; and when a crowd gathered Gwen was pushed to the rear where she couldn't see anything but a long row of pictures—abstracts—down a long snaky hall.

She woke when somebody put a thermometer in her mouth, straight out of the refrigerator. It was no-time, not dark or light, not late, not early. She could not even remember if the year bent toward Easter or Halloween.

Pressure bloomed suddenly in her gut. She barely made it to the toilet, still munching the glass rod. She filled the bowl with stained oil and walked carefully back to bed, rubbing her swollen abdomen for tremors. She had not wakened in the night when the baby thumped, nor once felt the long leg cramps which meant he had leaned on her femoral arteries. It came to Gwen suddenly that the baby must be dead, had smothered inside her overnight. By her bed, Gwen stood first on one foot, then the other, shaking herself in case he might rattle in her like a peanut. She laid the thermometer on the table, knowing it measured her cold terror. She thumped herself. Nothing thumped back.

"Time to eat!" said Ramona Plumpton, peeling a banana from her tray.

Gwen got into bed, pressing her belly with both palms.

A tall black man brought her breakfast tray. He said it was about six-thirty. She had nothing but juice and black coffee, which she must not drink until a nurse checked her temperature and said it was fine. "No labor pains?"

"No. And he isn't moving!"

"He's waiting for *you* to move him," she said with a smile, and marked a failing grade on Gwen's chart. Later a resident pulled the curtain around her bed and thrust a number of fingers into her, all the wrong size. He said they'd induce at nine o'clock. She played with that awhile: induce, seduce; reduce, produce. She folded out *Playboy*'s nude Playmate of the Month, also hairless, with tinted foam-rubber skin. There was an article which claimed Miss April read Nietzsche and collected Guatemalan postage stamps, preferred the Ruy Lopez in chess, and had once composed an oratorio. Miss April owned two glistening nipples which someone—the photographer?—had just sucked to points before the shutter clicked.

At nine, strangers rolled Gwen into what looked like a restaurant kitchen, Grade A, and strapped her feet wide into steel stirrups on each side of a hard table. The small of her back hurt. Gwen wanted to brace it with the flat of one hand, but somebody tied it alongside her hip. "Don't do that!" Gwen said, flapping her left out of reach. A nurse plucked it from the air like a tame partridge. "Regular procedure," said the nurse, and tied it in place.

Through a side door came Dr. Somers, dressed in crisp lettuce-colored clothes. He talked briefly about the weather and Vietnam while he drove both hands into powdered rubber gloves.

Gwen broke in, "Is my baby dead?"

Above the gauze mask his eyes flared and shrank. "Certainly not." He sounded muffled and insincere.

Gwen let down her lids. Spider patterns of light and dark. Caught in the web, tiny sunspots and eclipses.

Someone spread her legs wider. She felt strange cold things sliding in, one of them shaped like a mailed fist on a hard bronze forearm. The witches did that for Black Mass. Used a metal dildo. Gwen was not frightened, only as shocked as a witch to find the devil's part icy, incapable of being warmed even there, at her deepest. She cracked her lids and saw the rapist bend, half bald beyond the white sheet which swaddled her knees.

"*Fine,*" said the gauze. "*Just fine.*" He called over a mummified henchman and he, too, admired the scene. Gwen felt herself the reverse of some tiny pocket peep show, some key charm through which men look at spread technicolor thighs, magnified and welcoming. Now she enclosed the peephole, and through their cold tube they gloated over her dimpled cervix, which throbbed in rhythm like a winking pear.

Helpless and angry, she thought: Everything's filthy.

"Looks just fine," the henchman said, fidgeting in his green robe. Gwen wondered what the sister thought as she rolled an enamel table across the room like the vicar's tea cart. Full of grace? Fruit of *whose* womb?

Dr. Somers said, "There'll be one quick pain, Gwendolyn. Don't jump."

Until then she had given up jumping, spread and tied down as she was. Now she knew at his lightest touch she would leap, shrieking, and his scalpel would pierce her through like a spear. The sweat on her upper lip ran hot into her mouth. Sour.

"Lie very still now," said the sister.

The pain, when it came, was not great. If fluid spilled, Gwen could not tell, since the sharp prick spilled her all over with exhalations, small grunts, muscles she did not even own falling loose. "Nothing to it," Dr. Somers said.

She shivered when the devil took himself out of her.

"Now we just wait awhile." He gave a mysterious message to the sister, who injected something high in Gwen's arm.

They freed her trembly hands and feet and rolled her back to the room she remembered well from yesterday.

Everything, magically, had been shifted here—Klee, clock, her magazines and mysteries. Mrs. Plumpton had even sent a choice collection from her candy box, mostly chocolate-covered cherries, which the sister said Gwen couldn't eat yet. Overnight Jesus had moved very slightly on His cross and dropped His chin onto one shoulder. Yet His exhaustion looked faked. Forewarned, He awaited the shaking and dark. He was listening for that swift zipper rent in the veil of the tabernacle, ceiling to floor. Three days from now (count them: three) and the great stone would roll.

Gwen stared at the sister who helped her into bed. Was this the one who shifted the figurines? Did she carry under her habit, even now, the next distraught bronze who, when cued, would cry out about being forsaken?

Politely, Gwen asked, "You like your work here?"

"Of course. All my patients are happy. You should sleep now, Mrs. Gower, and catnap from now on. Things will happen by themselves."

Trusting no one, Gwen opened her eyes as wide as they would go. Her face was one huge wakeful eye, like a headlamp. "Is my husband outside?"

"Not yet," said the sister, smiling. "Can I get you anything before I go? No? And drink water."

The baby might have died from drowning. Unbaptized, but drowned. Gwen was certain she did not sleep, yet Dr. Somers was suddenly there in a business suit, patting her arm. "You've started nicely," he said.

She felt dizzy from the hypodermic. She announced she would not give birth, after all, having changed her mind. Her body felt drawn and she sat up to see if her feet had been locked into traction. Dr. Somers said Mr. Gower had come by and been sent on to work—there was plenty of time. He faded, sharpened again to say Gwendolyn was to ask the nurse when she needed it.

The next thing she noticed was a line of figures who climbed in her window, rattling aside the venetian blinds and straddling a radiator, then crossing her room and marching out into the hall. It was very peculiar, since her room was on the hospital's fourth floor. Most of the people did not speak or even notice her. A few nodded, slightly embarrassed to find her lying by their path, then drew away toward the wall and passed by, like Levites, on the other side.

One was a frightened young Jewish girl, hardly fourteen, whose weary face showed what a hard climb it had been up the sheer brick side of the hospital. Behind her came an aging athlete in lederhosen, drunk; he wore one wing like a swan's and was yodeling *Leda-Leda-Ledal-lay*. He gave Gwen a sharp look, half lecherous, as he went by her bed, flapping his snowy wing as if it were a nuisance he could not dislodge. A workman in coveralls climbed in next; he thrust head and shoulders back out the window and called to someone, "I tell you it's already open wide enough!" After much coaxing, the penguin followed him in and rode through the room on his shoulder, so heavy the workman tottered under the glossy weight. Several in the parade kept their rude backs to her. Angry, Gwen called them by name but they would not turn, and two of the women whispered about her when they went by.

It was noon when Gwen next looked at the clock. Richard had not come back. Instantly awake and furious, Gwen swung out of the high bed. She nearly fell. She grabbed for the metal chair—Good God!—something thudded in her middle like a pile driver. She felt curiously numb and in pain at the same time. She clumped to the doorway and hung on to the frame. There was a nun at a small desk to her right, filling out charts in a lovely, complex script.

"Going to telephone my husband," Gwen said. Her voice box had fallen and each word had to be grunted up from a long distance.

A chair was slid under her. ". . . shouldn't be out of bed . . . Quickly." The nurse balanced the telephone on Gwen's knees.

She dialed and Mrs. Gower said, "Hello?" Her voice was high and sweet, as if she had just broken off some soprano melody. Gwen said nothing. "Hello? Hello? Is anybody there?"

With great effort, short of breath, she said, "May I speak to Richard Gower? Please?"

"He's eating lunch."

Gwen looked at the far wall. A niche, some figurines, a lighted candle. She took a deep breath. When she screamed full blast, no doubt, the candle would blow out twelve feet away and across town the old lady's eardrum would spatter all over the telephone. But before she got half enough air sucked in, she heard, "Gwen? That's not you? Gwen, good heavens, you're not out of bed? Richard! Richard, come quick!"

Gwen could hear the chair toppling at the table, Richard's heavy shoes running down the hall, and then, "Gwen? Gwen, you're all right?"

Wet and nasal, the breath flew out of her. "You just better get yourself over here, Richard Gower. That's all," she wailed. "You just quit eating and come this very minute. How can you eat at a time like this?"

Richard swore the doctor said they had hours yet. He was on his way right now and he hadn't even been *able* to eat, thinking of her.

She told him to hurry and slammed down the phone. The nun was looking at her, shaking her headdress. She half pushed Gwen into bed. "Now you've scared him," she said gently.

Gwen shook free of her wide black sleeve. The next pain hit her and this one was pain—not a "contraction" at all. One more lie in a long line of lies. "Long-line-of-lies," she recited to herself, and got through the pain by keeping rhythm.

> *"One more lie*
> *In a*
> *Long line*
> *Of lies."*

On the next pain, she remembered to breathe deep and count. She needed fourteen long breaths to get through it, and only the six gasps in the middle were really bad.

By the time Richard trotted in, she was up to twenty-two breaths, and most of them were hard ones in the center without much taper on either end. He stopped dead, his mouth crooked, and Gwen knew she must look pale. Perhaps even ugly. She could no longer remember why she had wanted him there.

"Good," said Dr. Somers. "We were just taking her in."

Richard kissed her. Gwen would not say anything. He rubbed her forehead with his fingers. New wrinkles had broken there, perhaps, like Ramona's stretch marks. As they rolled her into the delivery room, Gwen saw that Jesus had perked up a lot, gotten His second wind. She closed her eyes, mentally counting her pains in tune. One and two and three-three-three. Four-four-four. Five-five-five. Words caught up slowly with the music in her head: Mary had a little lamb. Little Lamb. Little . . .

When they made her sit upright on the table so an anesthetic could be shot into her spine, Gwen hurt too much from the bending even to feel the puncture. They had trouble getting her spread and tied into this morning's position; she had begun to thrash around and moan. She could not help the thrashing, yet she enjoyed it, too. If they'd let go of me once, I'd flop all over this damn sterile floor like a whale on the beach. I'd bellow like an elephant.

That reminded me of something Dr. Somers had said—that in the delivery room most Negro women prayed. *Jesus! Oh, Lord! Sweet Jesus!* And most white women, including the highborn, cursed. Oh, you damn fool, Gwen groaned (aloud, probably). It's *all* swearing!

Oh, Jesus!

Oh, hell!

They scratched at her thighs with pins and then combs and then Kleenex, and Dr. Somers said that proved the anesthetic was working. Gwen fell rather quickly from agony to half-death and floated loose, broken in two at the waist.

"Move your right foot," said the doctor, and somebody's right foot moved. He explained she would be able to bear down, by will, even though she would notice only the intent to do so, and not feel herself pushing. So when they said bear down, Gwen thought about that, and somebody else bore down somewhere to suit them.

"High forceps." Two hands molded something below her navel, outside, and pressed it.

"Now," said the mummified henchman.

The huge overhead light had the blueness of a gas flame. She might paint it, staring, on a round canvas. She might call the painting "Madonna's Eye." She might even rise up into it and float loose in the salty eye of the Blessed Damozel like a dust mote.

Suddenly the doctor was very busy and, like a magician, tugged out of nowhere a long and slimy blue-gray thing, one gut spilling from its tail. No, that was cord, umbilical cord. He dropped the mass wetly on the sheet near Gwen's waist, groped into an opening at one end. Then that blunt end of it rolled, became a soft head on a stringy neck, rolled farther and had a face, bas-relief, carved shallow on one side. The mouth gave a sickly mew and, before her eyes, the whole length began to bleach and to pinken. Gwen could hardly breathe from watching while it lay loosely on her middle and somehow finished being born of its own accord, by will, finally shaped itself and assumed a new color. Ribs tiny as a bird's sprang outward—she could see their whiteness through the skin. The baby screamed and shook a fist wildly at the great surgical light.

Like electricity, that scream jolted Gwen's every cell. She vibrated all over. "That's natural," said Dr. Somers, "that little nervous chill." He finished with the cord, handed the baby to a man in a grocer's apron, and began to probe atop her abdomen. "We'll let the placenta come and it's all done. He's a beautiful boy, Gwendolyn."

The pediatrician she and Richard had chosen was already busy at another table. Cleaning him, binding him, piling him into a scale for weight. Dr. Somers explained that Gwen must lie perfectly flat in bed, no pillow, so the spinal block would not give her headaches. If she'd drunk enough water, as ordered, her bladder would soon recover from the drug. Otherwise they'd use a catheter—no problem.

The sister, her face as round as the operating light, bent over her. "Have you picked out a name?"

"No," Gwen lied. *She* needed the new name. *She* was the one who would never be the same.

". . . a small incision so you wouldn't be torn by the birth. An episiotomy. I'll take the stitches now." Dr. Somers winked between her knees. "Some women ask me to take an extra stitch. To tighten them for their husbands."

Stitch up the whole damn thing, Gwen thought. They were scraping her numb thighs with combs again.

". . . may feel like hemorrhoids for a few days . . ."

She went to sleep. When she woke, there was a small glass pram alongside, and they were ready to roll her back to her room. Gwen tried to sit up, but a nun leaned on her shoulder. "Flat on your back, Mrs. Gower."

"I want to see."

"Shh." The sister bent over the small transparent box and lifted the bundle and flew it face down at her, so Gwen could see the baby as if he floated prone in the air. His head was tomato red, now, and the nun's starched wide sleeves flew out beyond his flaming ears. A flat, broad nose. Gwen would never be able to get the tip of her breast into that tiny mouth. There was peach fuzz dusted on his skull except in the top, where a hank of coarse black hair grew forward.

Gwen touched her throat to make sure no other hand had grabbed it. Something crawled under her skin, like the spider who webbed her eyelids tightening all lines. In both her eyes, the spider spilled her hot, wet eggs—those on the right for bitterness, and those on the left for joy.

The Glory
of His Nostrils

≠

It never occurred to Tom Carter, on the night of June 30, 1969, that somebody's sanity might be running out, even while he sat at the supper table eating too much of Mae's chicken and mashed potatoes. Had he been picking a day to go crazy in, he might have offered Halloween; but all he was really wondering that night was how you could tell if you had an ulcer.

Leaning back in his chair, he said, "I've eat too much. You must have put real cream and butter in the bowl." Mae, who had intended to make potato patties from the leftovers, said nothing.

The heavy meal had left Tom too sleepy to walk downtown and work overtime, but he had to. Tomorrow was the start of the county's fiscal year. Some of the figures in his annual report still wouldn't balance.

"Don't be late," was all Mae said when he grumbled. She stationed herself in front of the television with a second glass of iced tea. When he got to the front door, she called after him, "Is it raining, by any chance?"

And Tom hollered back, "No. Not yet." And burped.

The air was hot and dry. For two weeks there hadn't been a drop of rain in Rich County. No stars showed overhead and the clouds which hid them were lumped and heavy.

"It's cloudy, though!" he called. "Looks right threatening!" He waited, but Mae didn't even suggest he carry an umbrella. The TV's already got her, he thought. She's already busy watching Dr. Casey save some alcoholic.

Tom waddled down his front steps feeling unusually stubby, short, and unappreciated, his paunch bobbing in advance of him like a large stuffed olive. He puffed past four houses on Locust Street before he came to the large blue-gray one where Wanda Quincey, widowed at Easter, now lived alone. Her house, black-shuttered, graceful, trimmed in wooden lace and embroidery, reminded him first of a lady's summer frock. Then it looked cool as a moonlit pond.

Quincey was just my age, Tom thought. He stopped, belched once, and leaned against the maple by the curb while he fished in his pockets for an antacid tablet. That was how he happened to be the last person in Richdale to see Wanda Quincey in her right mind.

As he later told it, the Quincey porch light came on while he was propped against the tree. The house looked real nice lit up, he thought, black floor and ceiling, that curly gray banister, the gray wicker furniture. Quincey had made sure that house was painted every other year, and paid the mortgage off besides. Much good it did him now.

Something live burrowed through Tom's belly like a mole bubbling down its tunnel. He found a loose tablet stuck to his pocket seam. Mae feeds me too much, always has, so I'll go straight to sleep and sleep till morning.

Just then the front door opened and Quincey's widow

came out onto her black porch, carrying a copper watering can, which she emptied over a tubbed elephant-ear plant. Tom said afterward it was just like a stage setting—the heroine moving deftly among her bright props, not knowing there was anything at all beyond the footlights, much less a neighbor full of digestive gas.

Watching her, he licked tobacco crumbs off the mint wafer and slipped it underneath his hot tongue. Onstage the widow bent, placing the sprinkler on the steps. She stretched, rubbed one arm, then fitted her back to a porch post almost exactly as Tom himself was propped in the dark against the maple.

Leaning back, Wanda looked up at clouds which were passing across the sky like rolling barrels, tanks, and cisterns. Tom could not tell much about her face, a black-and-gray shape on a black neck, but the rest of her was buttered glossy in the yellow porch light.

She ain't fat yet, thought Tom, and chewed hard on his mint. Lonesome, maybe. Hot night, empty bed. Tom did not feel a bit disrespectful thinking this, although he had known Wanda all his life. He had been one of the pallbearers at Quincey's funeral.

But in this moment he could look at her lighted shoulders, waistline, hips as though they belonged to someone else, some character conveyed to him by stylized movements, with the light deliberately turned on her this way, to produce exactly this brassy effect. She more or less asks for it, thought Tom, and it seemed to him she opened her thighs slightly to his gaze.

Suddenly her shoulders fell forward. Light slid up like a yellow collar on her neck. Her breasts dropped so far he thought she had abruptly tired of having them grow on her all the time, like tumors. She didn't look a bit like herself, Tom thought again, but like some actress in some sad play.

Wanda turned, her pale costume gleaming. Rear stage she exited and the porch light instantly went out.

Without knowing exactly how, Tom Carter was deeply moved. He was never able to tell this mixed part of it: the pity that nearly made him go knock on her door; and the glee that he was here, alive, unseen, full of his wife's fried chicken. Distended with gas and itchy from the tree trunk, he nevertheless felt no older than a bridegroom. He marched briskly to the courthouse, humming to himself:

"What 'cha gonna do when the meat gives out, Honey?
What 'cha gonna do when the meat gives out, Babe?"

The janitor said Mr. Carter was surely in a fine mood for somebody having to work extra time; and Tom said that was attitude. Attitude made all the difference.

At seven-thirty the next morning, wearing a plaid robe, Wanda Quincey walked onto that same front porch, picked up her watering can, and threw it into Locust Street straight at Greene's laundry truck. It fell noisily short and took a crooked bounce over the hood and past the windshield. Mr. Greene hit his brakes, which saved him from being spattered when the slung milk bottle broke; but lined him up exactly right for the rolled newspaper, which flew in his front window by his nose and out the other side. He drove away as fast as the old truck would go, and the more he thought about what had happened, the less he believed it.

Inside a week, though, the whole town believed. Wanda Quincey, who on June 30th had been as nice a woman as you could want, had waked up crazy the morning of July 1st. Since that date opened the county's fiscal year (and it rained, breaking a two weeks' drought, besides), it was easy to remember the widow's craziness birthday, and to keep track of the length and degree of her illness.

Tom told everybody he had seen Wanda on the eve of its onset and she looked queer to him even then. "Gave me such a turn," he said in the County Clerk's office, "that I got behind a tree, a maple, and stayed there till she went inside."

"She threw the thing *at* me," said Mr. Greene, looking flattered. "I don't know what to make of it."

Somebody talked the Baptist preacher into paying a call, but Wanda wouldn't let him inside and flared up the minute he said she was looking well. Grief was like that, the preacher concluded, and grief would pass. She didn't seem dangerous.

By the time Dr. Benjamin came to Richdale, Wanda Quincey had been crazy three years, one month, and a week.

He took a giant step off the train, skipping the porter's stairs, and in four huge strides was inside the station asking the telegrapher, "Have you called me a cab?" He slapped a small card through Pete's ticket window. It said:

Dr. O. B. Benjamin
(Courtesy Title Only)

"Uh, say you want a cab?" Pete reached automatically for the buzzer, which rang in the toilet-sized building two hundred yards away, and read the card twice. Courtesy—Dr. Benjamin loomed beyond the metal bars, six and a half feet tall, black-haired, black-eyed, with a mustache above his mouth which was almost curly. He looked, thought Pete, *florid,* a word he could not even define. He wore a ruby-red ring on his little finger and some rumpled flower—an iris?—in his lapel. Pete told him the Owens Cab Company would be right along.

"Just keep my luggage till I send," said Benjamin in his evangelist's voice, took one wide step outdoors, and had his foot lifted and ready when the taxi pulled up in front of him.

"What's the best motor hotel?" he said as he closed the door and slapped one of his name cards on the driver's leatherette shoulder. The driver plucked it down with one hand, frowned, and then shrugged.

"Rich's, I guess."

"That the only one in town?"

"Yeah." He offered to give back the card, but the doctor waved it away, showing his black watch with the white numbers on it. The taxi whipped out of the dusty parking lot, across the tracks, and through Richdale's two-block business district.

"How many people live here?"

"Couple thousand." He thought about the doctor's card. "We got a hospital, though. Forty beds."

"Always this hot in August?"

The driver nodded, but said personally he thought it was good for a man to sweat. Cleaned out his blood. He waited to see if that would bring any professional remark, but the passenger said nothing. Might be a book-type doctor, he thought, and wondered if he could be a college coach.

Just beyond the Pure Oil Station was Richmotor Inn, which was new, built of concrete block, and painted pink. As if he had been thumped on the breastbone, the doctor said "UH!" when he saw it, swung out, and threw two dollars into the front seat. "I've got some bags at the station. If you'll bring them in an hour, I'll double this."

"Yes, *sir,* Doctor," said the driver. He tucked the man's calling card into the sweatband of his hat and offered the doc one of his own. "So you can ask for me special anytime you want good service." He sat rubbing the steering wheel while the big man went into the Richmotor lobby, trying to decide if he should have offered extras right away, women or whiskey. A clerk and the stranger passed the window, crossed the lobby, moved out of his sight.

In the hall the clerk was asking Dr. Benjamin if maybe he was from the university? Had he ever been in Richdale before?

"No, I'm not. No, never have."

Chiropractor? Guy that made eyeglasses? Doctor of divinity? That seemed to tickle him. "No. Medicine."

What kind of medicine did he practice?

"I don't," said Dr. Benjamin. "Not anymore."

The clerk laughed pleasantly as he unlocked the room door, flicked on a light, started the window air conditioner. "Great to be retired so young."

"Not that," said Dr. Benjamin, handing him a tip. "Defrocked." He had to force the money into the man's suddenly taut hand. "I'm an abortionist. Or was. Not anymore, of course."

"Of course not," said the clerk. Not wanting to back away, he found himself edging sideways like a crab, at the same time smiling widely in case the doctor had made a joke. The doctor himself was smiling, whatever that meant. "You staying long?"

"I might."

The clerk took one despairing look around, seeing the room turned into surgery, the lamp relocated, carpet stained, unspeakable things dropped in the wastebaskets. ". . . nice visit," he said behind the closing door.

When the cabdriver heard about it, he parked the two suitcases outside Dr. Benjamin's room, knocked on the door, and ran without even waiting for his tip. This was not from disapproval but enterprise, and he whistled all the way back to the cabstand. Once, he had heard the perfect businessman would raise rats on household garbage to feed to minks. Then when he skinned the minks for fur, he could feed their bodies to the rats again. As soon as the cycle was working and both flocks breeding steadily, there would be only profits and no expenses. Now it seemed to Delbert Owens—the cabdriver—that from whiskey to whore to unlicensed doctor was a fair imitation of that chain, and he wanted Dr. Benjamin to see early that he wasn't, by nature, greedy.

He called up Christine and Velma and told them to be standing by and, just in case, called up the colored girl as well. Pete said the doctor could have got on that train in Washington, Richmond, maybe even New York; so he added some gin and vermouth to the box he carried in the trunk of his taxi.

When it was fully dark, he called up Dr. Benjamin, introduced himself again, and asked if he could do anything at all to make him feel at home. No? If the doctor was lonesome, he could maybe send over a very reliable friend he knew. . . . Well, listen, if it was variety he liked . . .

Delbert Owens hung up abruptly, shocked.

"What'd he say?" asked Pete from his ticket cage.

Delbert shook his head. "Said he'd seen so many female bottoms, they'd got to look like faces to him. Grinning, frowning, wrinkled, young. Not so young. Said these days it took a face to interest him half as much as a bottom used to. Said the next woman in his life had to interest him from the very top down. You ever heard anything like that?"

"That's really what he said? In just those words?"

"Well, no," Delbert admitted. "He was dirty about it, like Yankees always are."

Though no visitor had been inside the Quincey house for three years, the people of Richdale watched Wanda's actions almost as if she were truly living on a stage. Every morning she rose at six and turned on the upstairs bathroom light. Before seven, a kitchen exhaust fan churned out steam instead of grease—must boil her morning eggs, and hard as stone from the time it took. Thirty minutes after that, although she had a perfectly good sink piped into Richdale's municipal system, Wanda emptied her dishpan off the back porch, hung it on a nail there like a farm woman, and stood on tiptoe, stretching widely in the morning air. Despite her pose, nobody thought of crucifixions. They watched for the way she spread and flexed her fingers and rotated her wrist joints.

The neighbors whispered, "Limbering up for the telephone!"

And when Wanda Quincey went inside they edged toward their own parlors and hallways, waiting to see whose phone would ring today.

Wanda had called almost every adult in town at least once. She no longer opened the calls with who she was—people *knew*—but nowadays launched right away into her purpose. This was always a grievance, and it had something to do with her dead husband.

"Mr. Wheeler? I see by the paper you're thinking of running for constable. I'd like to know if you plan to keep a special eye on the property of poor widow women with nobody looking after them and taxes eating them to death? I never even knew till after Quince died how many people were walking through our yard, throwing balls, letting their leaves blow . . . their trash scatter . . . their dogs . . ."

The burden of Wanda's calls was how cruelly Quince had been treated all his life. Quince had kept this from her protectively, had been too much of a gentleman even to admit it fully to himself. His papers had showed Wanda much of the truth, her insight the rest. Evidence filled his desk: the misplaced insurance premium, canceled appointment, a bill for the dented fender no driver confessed, the stock which declined in value despite a friend's advice, that cardiogram showing a normal heart ten weeks before it clogged and killed him. His name had been omitted from the list of the Richdale High School class of '38. One year the city directory had him spelled as Quincy and another year Quinsy, which was worse. The pattern was obvious. Wanda could not imagine how she had been so blind.

In Quince's strongbox she found four receipts for magazine subscriptions which never came. The bank had numerous times marked him overdrawn when he wasn't. That time he spoke to the Rotary Club, his speech was garbled into Martian by the typesetter, and the news photograph printed above it was blurred and rather fierce. Thinking back on it, Wanda could remember it was Quince's sweaters which shrank at the cleaners, his accounts which were billed twice, the letters he carried to the post office which the post office lost.

No doubt about it, Winslow Quincey had been a saint, while the world tried to break him. Now, in his honor, she telephoned that world.

And how the world squirmed! "Wanda, honey, I wish I could talk more about it but I've got this dentist appointment. . . ."

"I have to leave this minute to open the pharmacy, Mrs. Quincey, but I'll be glad to check that old account for you. I think it was that laxative pill he took and that foot ointment? I'll make sure. . . ."

"I assure you, Ma'am, that we used the same process that we use for everybody. As a licensed mortician, I have certain standards. . . ."

"Yes, Ma'am. Two papers on the roof in the past three months. We'll speak to the boy about it. And of course we'll credit your subscription. . . ."

Between calls Wanda read and reread the Book of Job. She had torn this intact from her King James Bible, leaving Esther right next to the Psalms; and when she walked up Locust Street to town she carried pages 370 to 390 in her left hand and read to herself aloud. There was little traffic in Richdale, and drivers looked out for her as she jaywalked in front of them, hissing aloud, ". . . and hath burned up the sheep and the servants, and consumed them; and I only am escaped alone to tell thee. . . ." If anyone dared to touch his horn, Wanda Quincey would flap the thin Bible pages in the air as though God Himself were brushing at flies with tissue paper.

She carried Job with her to church, reading all the way there and back and during the sermon as well. The Reverend Snell, praying, raised his voice to cover her sinister sighing from the back row. . . . "They are destroyed from morning to evening; they perish forever without any regarding it. . . ."

That was where Dr. Benjamin first met Wanda Quincey, on the back row at Richdale Baptist Church. It was his first Sunday in town. He had come because he felt as bound to see the Southern Baptists as he would, in Mexico, the Aztec ruins. And he was enjoying himself, singing the hymns with such vigor that people were twisting around to stare.

At eleven-ten Wanda came in, reading strongly, and joined him on the last bench. Brown hair, he noticed, going gray at the edge, and milky skin. Though haphazardly dressed, wearing one silver earring and one pearl, she was so clean that her skin had the fragrance of a baby after its bath. Dr. Benjamin smiled toward that fragrance, but Wanda was reading. He thought about how that cheek would feel to his hand. He offered her a hymnal but she read on, not looking up. Beside him she muttered through the offering and special music by the choir; he had to reach across her to pass the offering plate to an anemic-looking old gentleman who rolled his faded eyes.

Just as Wanda finished mouthing, "When I washed my steps with butter, and the rock poured me out rivers of oil," he tapped her on one shoulder.

"Hush up," said Dr. Benjamin, so loud the minister forgot whom he was praying to.

Wanda's mouth opened and hung there. Pink, he thought. Moist. Tasting faintly of strawberries.

She nearly ran to the aisle. Job shivered in her hand. All the way from the bench to the vestibule, Wanda forgot to read, and had to start over at Chapter 1, having lost her place.

Monday morning, following the light, the fan, the water, the dishpan, the exercises, Wanda dialed the Baptist preacher and asked who that stranger was at church, the big man in the back row.

Mr. Snell was so startled not to hear her usual complaint about how Quincey's memorial money was being spent that his silence made Wanda think the line was dead. She hung up and dialed his number over.

"I said, Who was that big man on the back row in church yesterday?"

"Why, Benjamin, I think. He signed a visitor's card."

"Benjamin who?"

"That's his last name. A transient, I believe. No, I don't know where he lives."

After lunch Wanda walked to the Richdale Pharmacy for shampoo and talcum, reading Job's tribulations as she went.

"Yonder she comes," somebody said, giggling, on the courthouse bench. For a change Wanda *heard* it, although she had come to one of the best parts: "When the morning stars sang together. . . ." She looked up angrily, but it was only a boy, his elbows out at his sides like a pair of coat hangers.

The same thing happened half a block nearer town. Some high voice snickered, and Wanda looked into the squirrel-bright eyes of a blue woman under a velvet hat. She looked like a walking blood disease, and Wanda thought how old everybody was getting in her absence. The woman began a shrill cough and covered up the giggle. Wanda flipped a new page and pinned it with her thumb, reading, "Will the unicorn be willing to serve thee, or abide by thy crib?"

"Will he, indeed?" said Dr. Benjamin. He was in front of the pink motel, right at the edge of its parking lot, sitting in one of the bent fruitwood chairs which belonged in the lobby. "Good afternoon, Ma'am," he said, and touched one forefinger to his thick hair as if he might doff it all in her honor.

Wanda stopped on the sidewalk, her finger caught between the verse about unicorns and the one about peacocks and ostriches. "How dare you speak to me?"

"A poor substitute for the Almighty, no doubt," he said. His smile was the first Wanda Quincey had noticed in three years, and she thought it the size of a slice of watermelon. Through it he said, "I much prefer the Book of Ruth, myself, where widows behave more sensibly."

"Glean in your fields, I suppose," snapped Wanda, for she

wouldn't have him think she'd forgotten that part of the Bible she kept at home.

"You must be," he said slowly and thoughtfully, "really paranoid." He shook his head, his tongue clopping softly in his mouth. There were frown lines between his furry eyebrows.

She hadn't a thing to throw at him but twenty flimsy pages. "Mr. Benjamin . . ." she began coldly.

"Doctor. Dr. Benjamin. I'm an abortionist." He tried to hand her a card but she reared away.

"You ought to be locked up."

"I have been," he said. "If you'd dye your hair, you'd look younger. Everybody does that now. I do myself."

Wanda had started to walk on, reading firmly to blot the big man from her mind, and was disgusted to hear her own grand voice announcing, "THE GLORY OF HIS NOSTRILS IS TERRIBLE!"

Dr. Benjamin roared with laughter, throwing back his broad head until his own nostrils were opened to the sun like twin caves, and the bright light could shine all the way up onto the surface of his brain. Wanda walked rapidly from him down the street. Delbert Owens, who had been coasting his cab by them downhill in the dappled shade, scraped half the whitewall from two tires against the curb. "You all right, Mrs. Quincey?" he called when he had finally jerked free of the gutter. She read him some angry, incoherent verse.

When she came back from the pharmacy, Dr. Benjamin was still sitting in front of the motel.

Wanda tucked the paper sack tighter under one arm. She had not bought New Dawn Hair Color, but out of simple interest had opened one of the boxes on the shelf, taken out the printed direction sheet, and slipped that in with her purchases.

"If you'll come in," called Dr. Benjamin while she was

more than ten steps away, and loud enough to be heard all the way to the Baptist manse, "I'll offer you a drink."

Wanda began shaking her head without even looking at him. She shook it all the way reaching him, passing him, and going away; and by the time she got to the courthouse bench she was quite dizzy, and had to sit down. On the bench she read, several times, with growing strength, how "Job died, being old and full of days," and after Job was really dead enough, she felt like walking home. She thought it was a shame the coat-hanger boy had missed that fine conclusion.

That afternoon she made no calls. The lines were jammed with people trying to find out who Wanda was calling *now*. She locked herself into the upstairs bathroom and read the folder about shampooing in youth, which would last for forty-two days, with a mixture so powerful plastic gloves were supplied with every bottle.

That night her kitchen fan went on at seven, as usual, but nothing at all blew out except air. The fan whirled all night, forgotten and sent a pleasant little vibration up and down the neighborhood. One of the neighbors called the Quincey number just to make sure she hadn't fallen down the stairs and died, but hung up as soon as Wanda answered.

Upstairs, Wanda stood in her bedroom in the growing dark, unfastening the back buttons on her blouse. Her eyes flicked from the glass over Quincey's photograph to the glass in which she saw herself reflected. She wondered why the mirror switched her only from right to left but not from down to up. Some night, Wanda suspected, she might be reversed this second way also, and undress while standing on her head. She began her usual conversation.

"Quince," she said, and the portrait dipped politely in its

frame. "The queerest thing happened to me today. A man asked a crazy woman to come to his room for a drink. What do you think of that?"

Slightly muffled behind his dusty glass, Quincey said he knew exactly what such a man must have in mind.

"That's what I thought, too." She stepped out of her skirt. "And, Quince, it's been a long time since—well, since I felt that *idea* in anybody. You do understand, don't you? I don't mean to sound disloyal. But somebody else's thought, his thought about you, is almost like some garment. You can't help trying it on. Just to see if it fits."

Quincey's expression had grown rather ugly, as if he might push his face through the glass. "Did it fit?" he said.

"You're not supposed to talk," said Wanda, "except when I ask you questions."

She hung her blouse and brown skirt on the bedpost and turned so she could look over one shoulder at her mirrored back. The nylon clung nicely to her hips, she saw, and she wondered if Dr. Benjamin had thought as much when he watched her walking by. She decided not to mention that to Quincey.

From her nightstand he rasped suddenly, "What are you looking at?"

She said dreamily, "I've been thinking of tinting my hair. Red, maybe. Like a sweet-gum tree in the fall of the year."

"Maple is red," said Quincey, always a stickler for accuracy. "Sweet gums get purple. And no lady would dye her hair red."

"I'm thinking about that, too." Wanda unpinned her bun and the hair fell below her shoulders and tickled her spine. It was the color, she thought, of harmless brown garden snakes. "Quince, how old were you? In 1969?"

"Not but forty-five."

"And I was thirty-six." She wrapped a strand of hair around one wrist. Dr. Benjamin wore a black watch and a red ring. "We could have had babies, Quince, even though we did marry late. You know that? I wasn't too old." There was a rattle. "Don't vibrate, Quince. It scratches the table." She began brushing her hair.

"Children?" said Quincey. "Children to stay home with us when we got old?"

She whispered, "You didn't get old."

"Children to be nurses when we got sick? The way I stayed home with Mama till she finally died? The way you spent years shooting your papa full of insulin so he couldn't die and you couldn't live? We talked about all of that."

"Soon I'll be forty," Wanda said. She folded his stand down and stored him in a drawer. Then she yanked the petticoat over her head and studied herself in the full-length mirror, stripped down to brassière and pants. She could see that thirty-nine years of gravity had weighted her flesh—the stomach was not flat, the breasts no longer high. Everywhere, the cells of her body yearned slightly downward: shoulders, buttocks, even those folds hung under her chin and eyes.

I have begun, she thought, to fall very slowly into Quincey's grave.

Barefoot she padded out of her room, down the narrow stairs, and to her desk telephone. She asked the Richmotor Inn to give her Dr. Benjamin, please.

His voice burst in her ear.

Quickly she said, "This is Wanda Quincey, and I'd like to know who you think I am, asking me up to your room like that."

Now he said nothing. This bothered Wanda not at all, since silence had been tried by telephone subscribers all over Richdale. She leaned back in her chair and placed her naked feet on the desk top. Her legs looked very white and very long.

"If you want to see *me*," she said, and giggled suddenly.

He asked if she'd finished her reading yet.

"If you want to see *me*," she went on, "you can behave like a gentleman and come calling. I live at 402 Locust Street."

"Honey," boomed Dr. Benjamin, "do you like Scotch or bourbon?"

"I've entirely forgotten," she said, and hung up.

Shortly after midnight, August 18, 1972, a tall man with a package tucked in each armpit knocked loudly on the widow Quincey's black front door. When the porch light went on, he was seen silhouetted like something precious displayed in a gray box on a well-lit velvet lining. Old Mr. Wilkie was in his upstairs toilet at the time, wondering if he might have an enlarged prostate, and he saw the door swing wide to the visitor. For a minute it looked as if Wanda Quincey didn't have a thing on but her underwear, but then Dr. Benjamin bowed so deeply she was cut off from view.

The next day Wanda used the telephone only twice: to tell Richmotor Inn Dr. Benjamin was checking out; and to ask Delbert Owens to taxi over his suitcases and another fifth of Scotch. By then she had remembered which flavor she preferred.

All that week, people rode slowly up and down Locust Street to stare at the Quincey house.

Its shades and shutters and curtains were closed. After

supper, everybody living in the 400 block sat on his front porch and stared, and some invited friends to come stare with them, but no lights went on anywhere in the house. Even the kitchen fan had snapped down its door like an eyelid. Neighbors tiptoed and whispered in their houses. Still they could hear nothing. No scream, no voice. Not even a footfall.

"All I know," Delbert Owens said, in answer to the Sheriff's questions, "is that I carried him two suitcases and he walked me back to the cab for change. He didn't have nothing smaller than a twenty."

"And what did he say?"

"Said Wanda Quincey would never have lost her mind if she'd had a husband who shared more with her. His work, his business. Everything. I gave him the old wink then, but he didn't wink back. Said this town was no good for her, either, and looked at me hard."

"Town my ass. And that's all?"

"Said in some ways Wanda was better off when her papa was alive with the diabetes. Gave her a thing to do. Said she had even taught herself how to give him shots by sticking a hypo in an orange."

"No news in that."

"Would have made a good nurse, he said."

"And what else?"

"Nothing else. He was looking a little tired out when I saw him."

"But no blood on him anywhere? No cuts? No scratches? You didn't really see Wanda herself, alive?"

"I didn't see her. All he had was, low on his neck, one big red lump. He had a dent in it." Delbert pushed down his belt and scratched his navel. "A dent just like a tooth makes in a apple."

"Apple, orange, the hell with it," said the Sheriff.

But since his telephone was ringing off the wall with questions, he put on his badge and gun and drove his official car to Locust Street and knocked at the door of 402.

Wanda herself answered. She was wrapped in what was either some flowered robe or a twisted bedspread. Her face was flushed and the tip of her chin was scraped as if she had fallen face-first into a sandpile.

She said, "Good afternoon!" in that perky but vague way children speak when they have had a long fever.

"Wanda? You're doing okay, Wanda?" What really made the Sheriff stammer was the wealth of bright red hair, standing out from her head in all directions like a burning bush.

Wanda looked right through him. "You don't need to break it to me gently, Sheriff. Quince is dead. My husband is dead. I've suspected it for a long time." She gave a brilliant smile across his shoulder to whatever she was looking at.

"Ma'am, maybe you ought to . . . well . . . come with me now. See a doctor. Nobody's going to hurt you. We'll help you feel better."

"I've seen my doctor, and if I felt any better I would float right up over your head." She put her right hand on that blazing mop of hair and rubbed it gently. He saw that her feet were bare and a kneecap was showing which was bare, also.

The Sheriff didn't know what to do. He had no search warrant. Nobody had signed any papers to commit her. "Uh, Benjamin's staying here, is he?"

"Just till tomorrow. We're going to Chicago. Or maybe to San Francisco, where the bridges are. I'm going to take an interest in his work. I'm going to sit there and wait, and people will telephone me. I'm going to keep his papers in order."

She undid one corner of her robe and threw it back in place again in a very queenly fashion. It was a bedspread, after all; part of the fringe was showing.

The Sheriff tried to see beyond her and down the dark hall. "Maybe I could talk to him about that?"

She said haughtily, "Not unless you telephone first." Out of the folds of her flowered wrap she took a Sunkist orange and began thumping it from one palm to another. "I think that's all, Sheriff. Don't you?" She closed the black door with him still standing there trying to think of some crime to charge somebody with.

All the time Wanda and Dr. Benjamin waited in the depot for the northbound train, Pete tried to get Wanda by herself. He called the doc to the telephone, but Wanda decided to use the ladies' room just at that time. He insisted on carrying their bags personally, even though he knew it was bad for his bursitis. Loaded down, he walked at Wanda's elbow saying "Psst! Psst!"

"Honey," said Wanda to Dr. Benjamin, "I think Pete's talking to you."

"No, no. Just wheezing. Little cold." He loaded the suitcases on the wagon and rolled it over the depot yard by the tracks, to wait for the Silver Meteor.

"When you coming back, Miz Quincey?" he finally decided to ask in front of them both.

"Back where?" she said.

Pete could see Delbert Owens inching his taxicab across the big lot at zero miles an hour, hoping to hear what went on. Finally he parked it nearby and got out and sat on the hood and cleaned his fingernails.

Nervously, Pete said, "Here you was, just stopping off in Richdale on your way to someplace, and look what happened." He looked up at Dr. Benjamin, who now seemed seven feet tall or eight, and then around to see how close Delbert was if he needed him. "You going home now to your wife?"

"What wife?" Dr. Benjamin laughed so loudly it sounded as if trains were coming headlong in both directions. To Wanda he said in a whisper, "Don't stand too close; you'll get hurt," and, with his fingers, caught her right breast like some kind of handle and pulled her back from the tracks. Pete said it was the damnedest thing he ever saw.

When the train did come bellowing into Richdale, Pete had his only chance. Under its clangor and whistle and spitting, he yelled into Wanda's ear, "He's an ABORTIONIST! He's dangerous. Don't GO with him!"

Dr. Benjamin turned his broad head. "What's that?"

Wanda said, "Pay no attention, honey. Everybody in this whole damn town is crazy."

They climbed onto the train, Dr. Benjamin helping her with one gentle palm at her elbow and a quick pinch elsewhere. Pete and Delbert Owens just stood together in the parking lot, and waited to see the two of them show up in one of the lighted windows in a passenger car, like a tiny film frame in an old-time nickelodeon. When the pair appeared, they walked a little closer to the railway car.

They were lit by that pinpoint light travelers use to read without disturbing other passengers. First Dr. Benjamin came into its shine, and sat down in the plush seat near the window. Maybe he winked at them; Delbert said so, but Delbert was owed one. Pete was never sure.

Then Wanda knelt on the aisle seat beside him and lowered her face against his, so the light flared brightly on her red hair. The train jerked once, northward. She bent forward and brushed her nose against Dr. Benjamin's nose. The train groaned and moved.

The last they saw, Wanda was framed in that lighted rectangle, scrubbing her nose urgently against his big nose, like a speechless Eskimo in a flaming parka.

The Spider Gardens
of Madagascar

After the two cars parked, the state patrolman climbed out of his and opened both black doors of the Ford. From the roof, out of sight behind a chimney, Coker watched his teacher, and his preacher, then his Grandmother Barnes step out. Briefly they put their four heads in a cluster, sometimes glancing toward the house. Grandmother's white hair bobbed ahead down the front walk between two flat rows of pansies. He knew she'd had to drive fifty miles. He could figure out everything from their stiff parade. While the doorbell rang in the empty house, Coker thought about not going down at all, simply to get details.

But all four would just sit on the porch glider and wait for him. Or go indoors and telephone the neighbors.

Coker swung into the sycamore and climbed down his knotted rope to the kitchen door. Inside he called, "I'm coming," so they'd stop ringing the bell.

He didn't, though. He stood by the humming refrigerator and picked his scab. If they're both hurt, he thought, Daddy's hurt the worst. If one is dead, he's the one. If they were both killed, he died first.

Think how cool it would be to climb into the refrigerator and go to sleep with the butter and eggs.

He dragged open the front door. Instantly, their faces dropped. Grandmother's eyes filled up with water. "My son," said the preacher gravely, and dropped on his shoulder an arm of solid lead.

"Coker!" the teacher said with a sigh, and his grandmother yanked him against her and cried on his new haircut.

He said, "They had a wreck?"

More crying. The patrolman took off his hat before he nodded. "Your mother's in the hospital, son. She's going to be just fine."

He saw they were going to make him ask. "And Daddy?"

Grandmother's muffled words fell through his hair roots and dropped cold on his brain. "God took him to Heaven, Coker. You know what that means."

He knew exactly what it meant. His grandmother's bosom smelled like coconut. He feared he might vomit on it. Mrs. Markas, who knew the signs, said maybe Coker-honey ought to sit down. Their fingers nipped at him all the way to the couch.

There was a crowd of hiccups in his throat. From behind him, the patrolman said again, "Your mother is going to be just fine."

All Coker could see was the pipe rack he had made in Mrs. Markas's class and given his father for Christmas. He stared at it until the wood got soft. "Daddy was planning to drive," he whispered.

"Yes. Will was driving and this truck—it doesn't help to

think of these things. Your daddy would want us to think of your mother now. And look after her." Coker stared into his grandmother's wet eyes. "You can see her at the hospital tomorrow," she said, her white head bobbing. "I'm going to stay here with you until Lillian's well." Between Coker's eyes and hers, Lillian's existence bloomed. Her daughter. Coker's mother. His eyes said: *Mama was screaming at him just before the wreck,* and hers said: *Maybe so, maybe so, but it can't be changed.*

Mrs. Markas advised him to go ahead and cry. "You'll feel better, Coker, honey."

As usual, Coker knew more than she. In her class and the four grades before hers, he'd seen how little teachers knew— reading aloud their sweet books about family picnics and turkey dinners. If crying made you feel good, he'd be Santa Claus by now.

His chest felt bruised. Inside, his throat was swelling. Dead, he thought. All the time gone. Left me to grow up by myself. Left me with *her.*

His throat blew out like a frog's and choked him.

"See?" said the teacher as he began to moan. "You'll really feel better. When we can't change what's happened, we might as well cry."

He cried, instead, for unchangeable things to come. He was ten years old.

It was fifth-grade Science Project time. Coker had so little faith in books, Mrs. Markas asked him to bring in a shoebox of different rocks. "I know things are busy at your house," she said. "Isn't your mother coming home from the hospital this week?"

"She did. Yesterday."

"Oh. Now isn't that fine! I hope she'll soon be completely recovered."

"Yes, Ma'am."

He picked up rocks all the way home from school. Each time he found one larger, or whiter, or darker, he threw his previous choice away, so he had only one in his pocket when he got home. Grandmother Barnes tossed that one into their stony side yard when she was washing his pants.

"How was I to know it was an important rock?" she said when he reappeared in his jeans. "You've already been in to see your mother?"

"Not yet." He climbed on a chair to get the peanut-butter jar.

"Well, do that first. You know she lies there all day waiting for you to get home. Go tell her what happened at school today."

He spread several crackers. "Nothing happened."

"Go tell her that, then."

Outside his mother's bedroom, he crammed his mouth full, knocked, and rushed in with his cheeks puffed out like bladders. His mother lay in the very center of the king-sized bed, her eyes glittering, her broken jaw wired shut. She said between her teeth, "Coker, what took you so long?" Before he could answer, she was into a long buzzing speech: "I never know where you are anymore and you just come home when it suits you. I'm about to go crazy with nothing to do and nothing to eat that won't come through a straw. You can't imagine how blue I get. And now's the time we've got to draw together, Coker, you and me. Alone in this world. You are the only thing I've got left. And it's not fair to worry me going off wherever you choose and not coming straight home. . . . Are you listening to me?"

Coker chewed. It took a long time to get the crumbs wet and work the peanut spread off his gums. "I had to get stuff for the teacher. Science. At school."

She leaned toward him and pillows fell softly forth on both sides. "Tell me about it," she said, patting the bed. Through her blue lacy top he could see the tips of her breasts, brown as acorns.

"That's all."

"Maybe I'd help. I could make you a poster or paste things in a book. It would give me something to do instead of going crazy." She laughed and immediately quit laughing. "What shall we do? Mount butterflies? I don't think you're even listening. Here I am offering to help, and you just stand there chewing your cud like a cow." She had always nibbled at his father this way. Met him every day at the front door like some starved bird, her white hands plucking loose in the air. *How's the new bookkeeper? If you'd bring the books home, I could check up after her. Don't you look flushed, Will! Is it fever? I bet you didn't eat a thing for lunch. After I fixed it and wrapped everything to stay fresh. You just don't appreciate, do you? I just wish you'd married some woman who didn't care if you got so hungry your blood dried up and when you cut yourself shaving it would blow off your face like dust!*

Coker could see his father still, standing in the front hall, his eyes flicking from one side to the other. Sometimes his mouth would stay open. He looked like a fish deciding if he dwelt in air or water, and how to move next. Deciding he would rather be a fish than a cow, Coker let his own jaw hang loose so Lillian could see the half-chewed food. She was still complaining about the kind of mother he should have had, that let him run wild in the streets. He sat on her bed and let her talk herself into a few tears and then out of them again.

"Kiss me and go play," she finally said. Her cheeks were pink and her blue eyes shone. "Someday you'll be sorry you treated me like this."

He kissed her near the ear, trying to miss the discolored skin. She had been thrown against the windshield, bruised, and thrown back again, caught by her safety belt. His father had gone straight through the glass, and looped like a kite in a wind current, before he hit a pine trunk and broke and slid down. Coker had dreamed this scene so often he felt like he had been standing by the car when it happened. He even knew Daddy's mouth was open on one word, "COKER!" which meant, "Be careful, Coker, when I'm gone." Or maybe "Come with me."

Grandmother was waiting in the kitchen doorway, a glass of milk in her hand. "You wash that stuff down, and Coker? I'm sorry about the rock. Can you do something else? There's a toad in the yard. I saw him when I was burning trash. You might could find tadpoles in some pond, warm as it's been."

He didn't want a toad.

"Could you find cocoons? Or take down a few mud-daubers' nests. There must be a hundred under the house."

"What kind of bug is a mud dauber?"

"Bee or wasp or something."

He crawled under the back steps, ducking the ghostly touch of spider webs. The mud-daubers' nests were everywhere, long brick-red tubes of clay which clung to the wood like small organ pipes. He broke off a set of four. The next nest was brittle, shattered in his fingers, and spilled out a dozen black balls the size of buckshot. In the dust, Coker rolled one with his finger. It was a curled, dry spider. . . . He picked up a few more and pinched them to powder. Then he crawled out and went to find his grandmother.

"How come there's dried-up spiders inside?"

She was talking on the telephone and shook her head. "A little better, I guess. All things considered. You know Lillian's always had these nerves. She can't help it. Even when she was a little girl. Just a minute." She pressed her fat hand on the mouthpiece. "They eat 'em, I guess, Coker. Now run on. I'm busy."

Coker had never thought a spider had any enemies but people. A spider that didn't get stomped, he felt, would live to old age and die slowly and lazily in the sunlit center of its web. Should any bird eat a spider, that bird would choke from its poison and tickle, and fly straight ahead into somebody's window.

He carried two mud nests to his room and got out the six-volume *Picture Facts* set he got for Christmas but had never read. Frogs, toads, and birds—it said—would eat spiders. Also wasps and praying mantises. One wasp invades the burrow of the trap-door spider, paralyzes it with a sting, and lays an egg on the abdomen—which will hatch and feed on its still-living but helpless host.

Coker was shivering; he didn't know why. It wasn't from pity for the spider.

Carefully he broke open another of the hollow clay rods. More shrunken spiders spilled across his desk, sucked dry by larvae which had long since spread wings and flexed their narrow waists and broken free. When his grandmother called supper, he scooped it all into a drawer.

Grandmother had been crying. Her cheeks were patched with red, as if someone had stood near with a file and rasped here and there on her face.

"What's the matter?"

"It's nothing. Your mother's a little upset."

"She's always upset."

"If only you could understand, Coker. You will when you're older. She's high-strung. This accident . . . we have to be patient."

"Daddy was patient."

"He certainly was." She cried quietly, a paper napkin flat on her eyes.

(Daddy was patient and Daddy is dead.)

Grandmother stopped rocking on her heels and joined him at the supper table. "Eat while the gravy's hot." She leaned back, not eating with him. She seldom ate much at meals, though she was very fat. She ate all the time she was cooking and all the time she cleaned up, and out of her apron pocket all day long.

She gave a rustling cough. "Let me put it this way, Coker. If somebody had a weak leg all his life, we wouldn't blame him if he couldn't run fast—right? Lillian's got a weak nature, weak nerves. She had to go to a doctor half of last year—remember that? You don't get cured, exactly. You just keep a weakness from getting worse."

"That's what the doctor said? She was born with some weak part?"

His grandmother slapped more mashed potatoes on his plate and drenched them with chicken drippings. "I don't think," she said angrily, "that doctor had the first idea what was wrong with Lillian." She poured his glass too full of milk. "What did you decide about the mud daubers?"

"I decided on spiders."

"Spiders. H'm. Well. You'll have to be careful. Some of them . . ."

"Bite," he finished.

At lunchtime, Coker hid in the boys' toilet while his classmates thumped down the hall to the cafeteria. Tiptoeing, he found the school library unlocked. He had never liked it, but now that the room was deserted he had a sense of ownership, and marched around giving every globe a twirl. He looked up "Spiders" in the card catalogue, then located 595 on the shelves. For an hour he read. When the librarian came back, he checked out three books and hid them under his shirt; he didn't want his teacher to think she'd won some battle.

In Science period, Mrs. Markas wrote their topics in a long list on the board. Sue would paint oak leaves in a booklet, with different species at different seasons. Clyde was bringing his salamander and Becky her goldfish. Everybody groaned. They were all sick of Becky's skinny goldfish, which had also come to Pet Day and to Show and Tell, and had served as a model for Plastic Arts.

"And Coker Gibson," said the teacher, "is making us a nice rock collection."

"Spiders," Coker said.

The chalk squeaked once and stopped. "Spiders? What do you plan to do, especially, about spiders?"

"Everything."

Becky, who had made a career from the dime-store aquarium, bent over to giggle.

He stood in the aisle and kicked her desk till she hushed. "I'm bringing in webs. And spiders in jars. And egg cases. When spiders catch bugs, they suck them dry and live on nothing but juice. They can change skeletons and go on living. Some make parachutes and float out to ships at sea. Some spiders can walk on top of water. Some grow so big in South America they catch and eat birds." He sat down heavily and jarred his backbone.

The class was silent. Mrs. Markas finally wrote "Spiders" by his name and let loose a nervous laugh. "We certainly don't want any of *those!*" she said. "You must be sure to let a grown-up help you, Coker, so you don't get hurt." She drew a spider (with only six legs) on the board and sketched in an hourglass on its back instead of its belly. Coker knew what it was.

"Don't worry," he said firmly. "My father will help me." When Mrs. Markas turned with her mouth open, he only stared at her, smiling. She hesitated, then let it pass. He guessed she would call up his grandmother tonight and discuss how best to help him. While she was writing the next name, Coker hissed over his shoulder to Becky, "Don't you want a water spider to go in your goldfish bowl?" She did not answer.

Going home that afternoon, he saw hundreds of spider webs he had been walking past all his life. Some looked like hammocks, others like sheets of silk; and the great wheels which floated between bushes, said his book, were the work of orb weavers. A large black-and-gold spider hung in the center of one, like a brooch pinned on a woman's hairnet. When the wind blew, she rode the billowing web in and out as if even empty space could breathe.

Coker half ran home so he could watch his mother's face when he called, "My Science subject is spiders! Want to help?"

Lillian pressed into the headboard of the bed, her closed teeth showing. "Spiders! Lord, no! What kind of thing is that for the school to make you study? What good will it ever do you to know about those nasty things? I don't see a thing wrong with wildflowers. Or birds. Couldn't you put a feeder outside my window and study birds? They'll be building their nests this month and it would give me something to do. Not that you care whether I lay here all day. . . ."

He ran out of her room, not listening but singing over and over in rhythm:

> *"Why did the fly*
> *Fly? Because the spider*
> *Spied her.*
> *Why did the fly*
> *Fly?—"*

"You come back here while I'm talking to you, Coker Ray Gibson!"

He swayed downstairs to his tune. Why did the fly fly? Because the spider spied her. . . . That was one thing about Lillian's broken jaw. Bound as it was, she couldn't really scream at anybody in the old way. The doctor had to give her special tranquil pills, Grandmother said, because of those unscreamed screams. Last year she'd taken them, too, as an outpatient. For weeks Coker had thought this term had something to do with her saying so often, "I am out a patience!" Lillian was always out a patience with weather, bills, all neighbors. Arched hairs about her eyes which grew faster than anybody could pluck. The lack of simple appreciation in this world. And Coker.

Once, her patience all gone as usual, Lillian went to P.-T.A., and when Coker interrupted a talk she and his second-grade teacher were having, she slapped him in the mouth. Then she began to cry and the teacher didn't know which one she ought to comfort. After that, Coker stopped bringing home notices about P.-T.A.

Some days, too, Lillian would set out to "make everything up to you, Coker." Those were the worst of all. The dining-room table would wait for him, sagging with cakes in two or three flavors, and his bedroom floor would be waxed so slick he had to walk across with care. Usually there were flowers all over the house—on windowsills and tables, standing in vases and jars and detergent bottles. Once, Coker found a rosebud jammed into every spigot. Daddy's and Coker's chairs in the dining room would be lined with bed pillows, the table set with linen cloth and place mats and napkins and rows of extra forks, with candles burning at just the right height to blind them as they ate two meats, and baked dishes, and vegetables with sauce poured over them, and soup you could see clear through. They would both rave, would praise her, would eat till they bloated; but none of it would do. Never could they eat enough, marvel enough, be grateful enough. In the end, Lillian would run upstairs to cry, the whole house full of dirty dishes, candle wax, wilting flowers. "What did I do?" Coker used to wail. "What did I say to make her cry?" His daddy would grip him inside his hard, warm arm. "It's not your fault. Not anybody's fault. And Coker?" Daddy would make him lift his face. "It isn't her fault either."

He was sorry he had allowed himself to remember that. His father's voice was so real inside his head, he could have sworn it had just poured, living, through his ear. Instead of rising, by magic, inside his brain. Coker began flapping his arms and leaping to blot out that magic.

As he went dancing through the back door (Why did the fly fly? Because the spider spied her), his grandmother called, "That's all the time you're spending with your mother?"

Still reciting, Coker scooted at speed under the back porch and fell belly-down in the cool dirt. It smelled as if a light rain had just ended. He lifted up a board, and hard-shelled bugs fled toward the dark. There was a web overhead with a fragment of brown leaf in it. Coker broke off an anchor line and felt the sticky silk near its base. He reached for another.

The sudden burn on the tip of his forefinger made him jerk back. He drew it close to his face and, in the dimness, could barely see the pinprick where the pain began. Under his eye, the pad of that finger turned numb and his skin seemed to harden down toward the knuckle. The web trembled. He saw a pale brown spider race along one of the threads and hide in the brick pillar. No widow, then. Coker tried to bend his fattened finger but it seemed to be turning to bone. Sticking it deep in his mouth, he sucked hard. He sensed this was an important moment, like those when Indians cut themselves in brotherhood and pressed their wet wounds to each other. He slid near the stacked brick and found the spider, drawn back in a hole in the mortar. She should have been watching him through many eyes, but in the gloom he couldn't count. Coker slid out into the sunny yard, certain that—behind him—the spider had already begun to reweave the framework of her web.

Sucking his swollen finger, he wandered through the large back lot. Grass and dirt in patches, unpruned trees, tangles of vetch and dandelion, privet which had grown into trees, an arbor with its back broken under scuppernongs. There were funnel webs in the weeds and now and then a long silk cable strung so far he had to follow its lead to find the woven snare. Sometimes he could see the folded, silk-lined leaf in which some spider held her trapline and waited.

From his room, Grandmother called out the window, "What's ailing your finger?"

"Nothing." He asked her to throw down his red library book and, grumbling, she unhooked the screen and dropped the book into his hands. Coker stuck it in his belt, climbed his knotted rope, and slid onto the narrow platform he had nailed in the sycamore. He had not read far before he came across the spider gardens of Madagascar where—in the nineteenth century—spiders had been raised to harvest their tough but delicate silk. He had never heard of Madagascar, a red-earth island which (the book said) broke off thousands of years ago from the coast of Africa.

Coker stared from his tree into the wide backyard, its red Carolina clay worn in places as hard as brick. From where he sat, it seemed that every gleam and glisten was the home of spiders who belonged to him, his whole garden ashine with their handiwork. He whispered, "Madagascar," and nipped dreamily at his aching finger.

Then, by will alone, he broke his Madagascar loose from the continent and shoved it out to sea. He leaned into the trade wind which blew smartly through his sycamore, and when Grandmother called him to eat, her voice was almost lost in the pounding surf. There were dark Africans everywhere, barely out of sight in the tangled vines, winding silk strands onto bamboo spindles. Some of them hummed at their work, like bees.

Finally, with one great swoop of his rope, the King of Madagascar swung onto the mainland. Behind him he could hear the blue lapping of the waves and the high sweet whine of a thousand spinnerets.

When Coker was five, the whole Gibson family had come under siege. He could still remember that fear. Some of it had stayed in the house, under the stairs and in the basement, soaked in like stain where no air or light could reach.

The siege began when a parked car on a sloping street shook free of its brakes and drove itself downhill and through the plate-glass window of his daddy's appliance store. "Insurance will cover it," Daddy said in the hall as soon as Lillian would allow him to speak. He hung up his coat and did not see—as Coker did—the quick blanching of her face, nor hear her whisper on the way to the kitchen, "I wonder why They did that?"

Soon Coker could tell that, during the day, his mother heard sounds too dim for him to hear. She would be tying his shoes and suddenly her head would tip back, listening, her neck as hard as the bough of a tree. He was called indoors when people passed their house, and backed against Lillian's legs to watch through the curtains till they were out of sight. Sometimes he woke from his nap to find her sitting guard by his bed, a broom upright in her hand. One night he dreamed animal men were meeting in his closet, each with teeth like the prongs of a dinner fork. He screamed; and when Lillian came to hear his babblings about the closet, she threw all his clothes out onto the floor and, by the time his daddy came, was on her hands and knees rapping inside for secret doors.

Then she went away for two months and came back with some kind of doctor's pills that dulled her hearing, so she could no longer tell enemies were rustling the shrubbery or breathing behind doors. Coker then worried that the attack might come by surprise, so he tried to listen alertly as she had; until sometimes he, too, could hear Them. After a while he forgot, and They left to lay siege to families in other houses.

Now that he was ten, Coker understood They were magic enemies inside Lillian's head, the way Daddy's remembered voice rang so real in his own. But why couldn't Lillian shut them off by will? He could rid his own brain of anything by vigorous running and yelling. Sometimes he wondered if those medieval people in Taranto, Italy, shown in his book bitten by tarantulas and thus hurled into frenzied dancing, did not thus clean their minds down to a healthy blank. After the accident, he even asked his Grandmother Barnes to buy a tarantella record for Lillian's phonograph, but she never did.

Early in May, Lillian was strong enough to come slowly downstairs on aluminum crutches and prop her cast on a hassock and watch television. Her face now was barely dingy with bruises, and her yellow hair grew dark brown near her scalp.

"Here's this good quiz show, Coker. Come watch it with me. We always used to have such a good time watching programs together."

As long as Coker could remember, Lillian had been claiming they used to do this thing and that, none of which he could ever recall. Perhaps that was magic, too.

"I've got to work on my project," he said from his card table in the corner. He had lacquered various spider webs and mounted them on pasteboard. This had taught him that when a web was not snug against the backing, cutting one foundation line would cause the whole thing to disintegrate. In a fishbowl closed with wire screening, he had imprisoned two spiders, a wolf and a crab, the latter able to change colors and match any flower it sat upon. Coker had been feeding them lightning bugs and moths, but his real hope was that one would attack the other while he watched.

"What's in that jelly jar?"

"Egg sac." Inside, perhaps, there were already hundreds of spiderlings, shedding their first skin and growing tiny claws.

When they tore their way out, Coker would carry them outdoors and watch them throw out their first silk, like parachutes, and be windblown all over Madagascar.

Lillian said to her mother that the boy was getting creepy. Spiders. That was all he talked about anymore.

"Maybe he'll go into science. A doctor."

"God, I hope not!" Lillian twisted her mouth. "All they give you is words and sugar pills. I need to get away from doctors. Soon as I'm well, Coker and I ought to take a little trip."

"The beach, maybe," said Grandmother, turning all her wrinkled fat upward in a smile. "It would do you both good."

"New York. I've never been to New York. I wouldn't mind living there."

"What would Coker do in a place like that?"

"For goodness' sakes. Art museums, zoos. Central Park. You're just like Will. He never liked big cities." With her remote-control button, Lillian flipped around every TV channel on the dial. "I'd have been happier in a big city, I know that much. I told him often enough. Not that he cared."

Grandmother frowned.

"In New York schools, they probably study space and physics, things like that. Coker could go to a planetarium." On TV a man in a spangled suit was playing the piano. Lillian turned it off. "You should have made me keep on with music lessons."

"You wouldn't practice," Grandmother said. "You used to hold your breath."

"It was your job to *make* me." Suddenly she shivered. "Coker, can't you keep that mess in your own room? I can almost feel things crawling on my skin."

"All right." That's why he hadn't been able to keep the dog, or the cat, or the canary bird. They gave off mites and fleas into the air. As he carried his project upstairs, Coker heard the women arguing about whether Lillian had taken her last pill at the right time.

Late in the night, coming back from the bathroom, he heard her crying softly in her wide bed. He tiptoed in. "Mother?" She reached out her long fingers and pulled him on the bed against her chest. His own sudden need to cry smothered him.

"Will's dead," she whispered. "What will we do?"

He didn't know.

"Tell me you love your mother."

He told her. Something burned sharp in him, like the sting of venom piercing through his chest wall. He could not tell whether it would kill him or change him to something marvelous. "I do love you, Mother, I do!" he cried, digging his face into her neck.

"I'm so lonely, Coker. And can't sleep. Stay here awhile." She helped him into her bed, lacing his fingers with hers. He lay alongside, staring at the black ceiling. His feet reached only to her knees, one of which was cold and hard in its plaster cast. He thought about Christmas morning till his eyes got wet.

Near his ear she said, "We've got to get out of this house, honey. Make a new life. Everything's going to work out for us now. I'm getting well in lots of different ways, Coker. You're going to be able to see a lot of difference in me as the weeks go by."

"O.K." All day Christmas, Lillian had laughed. Sat in his father's lap to light the new meerschaum pipe. The picture, by magic, flared up in Coker's head. He squeezed her fingers.

She jerked his. "Is that all you can say?"

"Whatever you want, Mother."

"Well, don't you even care? Wouldn't you like that? She rolled away, the broken leg left like a dragging anchor near his bare foot. Into the pillow she said, sighing, "Everybody's so hard to please. I know plenty of boys would get real excited about living in New York with an elevator right by their front door. I guess you wouldn't care if we lived on the dump and you had to wear feed sacks to school."

He slid to the edge of the mattress.

"Plenty of mothers could lean on their sons in a time of grief. Talk things over with them. Make plans." She groaned. "If they'd left me in the car a little longer, I might have burned to death. Sometimes I'm sorry they pulled me out."

"I'm not sorry," he said loudly, getting out of her bed. "I'm really not, Mother. But listen, why can't you? Why can't you? Why can't you?" He could not find the right end to his question; there was no word in the language for it.

He ran into his own bedroom, closed the door, and stared straight at the blazing bulb in his lamp. His eyes stung. When he walked to the window, the glare stayed with him and turned the glass opaque. Beyond it, wakeful spiders fed from their silver nets. When Coker's eyes adjusted, he thought he could see their strands like thin Christmas tinsel.

He tried hard to remember Christmas, but it was nearly Mother's Day. He dragged the glass cookie jar from under his bed and into the light. Under its lid of wire screening, a black spider turned in her web till the lamplight gleamed on the red hourglass low on her fat belly. Twin drops of blood. Coker watched her weave shut the capsule in which her eggs were stored. The silk wrapping was spun tighter and tighter and thicker and thicker. Satisfied at last, she backed into her silken tunnel in the core of her web and looked out where her egg case hung like a small world in a small, strung universe.

Someday soon, Coker was going to have to decide where he would turn her and her children loose—in Lillian's room, or his.

Benson Watts Is Dead and in Virginia

After I died, I woke up here.

Or so it seems. Perhaps I am actually still dying, locked in that darkness between one breath and the next, still wearing tubes which leak from my nostrils and drain that long incision. My wife may even yet continue to bend over the high bed to catch the next beat of my heart while the blood jar is ticking down, like a water clock, into my veins. Perhaps that last hospital scene is the only scene and all the rest is a dream in passage.

But the room and her melting face clicked off, I think. Then the smells went. She was saying something; I could still hear that—I stopped hearing it. I unbloated and the queer whistle in my breathing stopped. I could no longer tell the pain from cold. All my circuit breakers opened and sensations blurred. Someone set fire to my hand but it barely tickled.

Through all this, my mind was clearer and more finely tuned than it had ever been. I treasured that clarity, though it had less and less raw material to think with now. I thought: I must withdraw into my brain and hide—there's nothing left outside.

So I did. I backed into my brain farther and farther and got smaller and smaller the deeper I went, until I fell out the other side.

And woke up prone in this yellow grass. The color is important. When they rolled me back from surgery, it was May.

At first I didn't dare move. If I lifted my hand, it might fall through the air and drop back onto a starched sheet. I could not tell what was still attached to me and might clatter if I stirred.

The place where I lay was so . . . so ordinary. A sky as blue as a postcard. Between it and me, one tree limb: oak. White oak, I thought. The grass felt like all grass. When a cricket bounced over my head, I knew for sure we were a long way from the recovery room; they would not recover me. I sat up. I was on a sloping postcard meadow. At the bottom, a narrow stream. Willows. I touched my abdomen, which should have been hot and painful. Dacron trousers instead of gauze. Not mine, though. These were new.

Around my left wrist hung a small bracelet and a yellowish tag which looked like the ivory sliver off a piano key. On it, carved, was the following:

TO AVOID G.B.—
1. Dwell, then travel
2. Join forces
3. Disremember

Very carefully, I got to my feet. It had been a long time since I could move without pain. The cool wind was a shock and made me clap both hands to my head. Bald as an egg! Not even a prickle, a wisp, a whisker. Otherwise I was myself as I had been before the intestinal cancer, even a little younger. I tried to guess by flexing muscles, checking where pounds were gone, feeling my smoother face. A little beard starting down the cheeks. I thought I might be forty again, or maybe less. I tried out my voice. Normal. For practice, I said aloud, "Well, it sure as hell isn't Heaven," and my laugh was normal, too—forced, but even that was normal. I took a few steps, then ran downhill and splashed into the water in a pair of shoes I had never owned. Everything normal. A bright September day and I was alive in it.

Yet there was something. There was something wrong with my mind. Too quiet up there, not enough panic, too small a load of bewilderment, not even enough curiosity. Earlier I said of the tree limb, "White oak, I thought," and that wasn't right. I didn't *quite* think. This was spooky. It was more as if Something thought in me. I felt the words were moving by their own choice through my head the way air bubbles slide down the bowel.

I began walking along the stream bank waiting for—I don't know. For my head to clear? I felt aged forty from the neck down. I waited for that age to rise and cover me like water.

I was in Texas when I died. These hills and fields and meadows looked more to me like—what should I guess?—like Virginia. I said this over and over, aloud, "I'm dead and in Virginia," trying to make the sentence taste like mine. It never quite did.

Now and then, beside the stream, I would spot hoofprints. Cattle? Or deer? I saw nothing else alive except me, that cricket, and dozens of yellow birds on quick and nervous flights. Ricebirds in Virginia? They fed off tall stems and some stunted bush with brown catkins on its twigs. I jangled my wrist tag. I'd worn a bracelet there in the hospital, too, with my name spelled out in beads like an infant's. WATTS. Benson Watts. Ben.

I got the first pain, under one ear. Ben Watts. 226 Tracy Avenue . . .

I got the second pain, a needle, higher. I rattled the tag. *Disremember,* it said.

Crossing the stream, I noticed for the first time I was traveling in the direction it flowed—there! You see how my brain was? Unobservant. Unconcerned. At the water's edge was a stretch of pale sand. Beyond that the mud was like milk chocolate. More yellow grass grew on both sides to the edge of trees just turning from solid green to red maples and yellow hickories. The scattered pines were thinning their needles for fall.

I rounded a bend. To my right the land dipped off, and the water turned and ran downhill faster to empty into a long lake I could not see the end of, maybe half a mile wide. Its surface was very still with a skim of reflections. As I got closer, I knew what was wrong with this scenery, so ordinary and yet so unreal; and it came from absence. Everything I expected to see did not appear. No boats or motors, no fishermen, dogs, garbage, foam, signs, fences. No plastic bottles drifting near the shore. My head was aching. The sun was too harsh on my peeled scalp.

Near the water I glimpsed a small house, almost a hut. *Déjà vu.* I spun to the southwest to see if the Fitchburg Railroad skirted the lake. No. Yet it was his house or nearly like it, built beside the pond a hundred years ago for less than thirty dollars. Built yesterday. I began to run through the ripening grass. If I was back in time, was Thoreau inside? Writing in his journal? Or was it possible that each of us died away into our own personal image of serenity and would be tucked there forever like something in a pocket?

Running made my head worse. But that gut I had cursed for a year was now so new and strong I thought it might be turned to gold or silver, and I ran with both palms pressed there to feel each strand of muscle move.

The wooden door was half open, heavy on its leather hinges. I jumped a low stone wall and ran up the path.

One room with an earthen floor, a smaller one beyond in which I could see strings of onions, peppers, and bean pods. I touched the table, chair, bunk, saw that high shelves on both sides of a fieldstone hearth reached over my head. They held a set of books, maybe a hundred, all with the same green binding. I called out "Hello!" to more absence. Nobody answered; though there were ashes in the fireplace, not quite cold, and the charred spine of a book which seemed to match the others.

There was no dust. Under the bunk I found a stack of empty picture frames, white canvases, a wood box of paints and brushes, and I could see the clean squares on one wall where somebody's pictures had hung. There were no titles on the books, and when I pulled one out I found each page was lined but blank—the other books were the same. This time something happened that I expected; I found pen and ink on the bottom shelf.

To enter the back room I had to stoop. It was a pantry with a board floor. Cured hams were hanging from the ceiling over a flour bin. Crocks of meal and dried beans in sacks were under a table on which apples, potatoes, yams, pears, green tomatoes lay in neat rows. One high shelf held what looked like scuppernong wine in gallon jars. The wood bin was behind the door, full of oak logs, with a sack of cedar kindling nailed outside. The pantry was dim and its odors thick as fog.

I laid the wood over the andirons. Matches had been left in a tin by the hearth, and after I lit the lightwood I rummaged in a second strongbox where small jars of spices were jumbled, some without labels. I read once that if a man eats nutmeg his urine will smell like violets. Perhaps I will try it.

Slowly the oak bark caught fire underneath, curled off, till the log smoked and finally burned. Beautiful was the fire. Its color moved and changed. I sat before it, watching for the sudden lick of blue which would reappear in a new place. So long as I stared into the flames, my head did not hurt. When there were coals, I slid three sweet potatoes in to roast and sat on, dreaming, sometimes tapping the log with a poker so sparks would leap off and shower onto the dirt floor. I must have sat that way for hours.

But the potato hearts were still raw when I peeled and ate them. I rolled the thickest log across the floor and heaved it into place. Then I went to bed though it was barely dark.

In the night I woke to hear rustling beyond me, something large scraping its hide between a bush and the wall of my house. There were no windows. In the red firelight I found the poker and carried it with me and swung open the heavy door. A large deer moved down the path, stepping as carefully as if he had made it, so heavily antlered that he seemed to be holding up an iron grille by stiffening his neck. He bent and drank from the lake, snuffled lightly, moved off along the water's edge. As soon as he passed, the frogs that he left would sing out again, so I could follow him through the dark long after he was lost to sight.

It was the same deer. I put the poker under my bunk with
the paints and brushes. Only when I was settled and warm
again and had closed my eyes against the glow of the fireside
did I wonder: What does that mean? *Same* deer?

I knew suddenly it must be very dangerous to sleep. I
might slide back. My gut would reopen; some bastard in a
white coat would whisper, "He's coming out of it." I could
almost see my wife hunched in her chair, the brown rubber
tubes in her hands, waiting for me. And there was a drop of
borrowed blood, halfway down, hung there till my arm would
be under it.

But in spite of my fear I went to sleep and when I woke up,
I was still here.

2

In the morning I could not remember the deer. I could
remember getting out of bed in the dark, but not why. I ate an
apple, found coffee beans and an old-fashioned hand grinder,
and at last boiled the grounds in a cooking pot. The brew was
thick and scummy, but its smell was magnificent. I remembered I'd had no cigarettes for two weeks, no solid food for
longer than that. When I picked up the apple, saliva ran down
my throat in a flood, and I felt my nose was twitching like a
dog's.

I had dreamed about a deer. That's it. In the dream, an old
stag came into this house and offered to carry me across the
lake on his back. He spoke in rather a high voice for so large
an animal. He told me that when many deer swam the lake,
each rested his head on the haunches of the one in front, and

since the one behind did the same, they suffered no trouble from the weight. He said the whole line swam for the far shore with all speed in this linked position, to reach land before being befouled. He would be lead deer on this trip, he said, and would carry me himself.

No. The headache started.

No, there had been a real deer, outside. I saw him by the lake. It was hard to remember the simplest details. Was it a doe, a fawn? I had never seen a deer this close before—that much was certain.

I grabbed one of the green ledgers and began to write down who I was and how I got here and that the deer was real. It was hard to write. My head felt as if something had come loose inside and was banging the bone. I read the entry twice, until I had it all straight and in order. Every day I would do this; every morning I would set down the previous day and read all the earlier entries. This would be good training for my mind, which, I now thought, had suffered oxygen deprivation there at the end. At the beginning? Whichever it was.

My name is Benson Watts and when I died in Houston, Texas, I was sixty-five and had grandchildren—none of whom I liked very much. I also had thick gray hair and brushy eyebrows. When I told my namesake grandson I looked like John L. Lewis, he didn't know who Lewis was. Now I'm twenty-five years younger, in Virginia, and my scalp is like orange rind, nothing but skin and pores; and I don't remember Lewis too well myself except for the eyebrows.

He might have been a principal in some school where I taught. He had the face for the job. For years I taught U.S. and world history in high schools all over Texas, for peanuts, because that left my summers free. Summers I read books, collected stamps, built halves of sailboats in the backyard, took auto trips, sold Fuller brushes (once), and encyclopedias (four times), coached Little League, tried pottery and built my own kiln, got divorced and remarried, and made notes for the book I would someday write on the Cherokee Indian in North Carolina. Here I am at last, dead and in Virginia, with a pen and inkpot and one wall of blank paper handy, and all I can remember is Tsali and the Trail of Tears. Some joke.

Once, too, I thought I might go to graduate school and write a book on the Dark Ages, on the flickers of light in the Dark Ages. By 1969, I thought we might be edging into the shadow of some new darkness, and without a Church to persevere. I taught myself Latin so I could read illuminated manuscripts at Oxford instead of translations in Texas libraries. *Illuminated* manuscripts. What a good phrase! But I did not write that book, either, and now I cannot call up a single Latin root.

All I can easily remember are random facts about myself, which don't amount to much. Trivia. The substance is missing. Let me write down the details.

Texas is bigger than France. There are four or five Texases to be born in—mine happened to be Beaumont, four years after the Spindletop oil gusher blew in. There might have been 10,000 people there then; the city multiplied itself by twelve in my lifetime. I stopped liking Beaumont when it passed 20,000, finished at Baylor, and started teaching history to conceited teen-agers who—if they owned the world and Texas—would rent out the world and live in Texas. That may be why Lyndon Johnson went to Washington, to see for himself how unlucky everybody else was. He stayed gone a long time.

Most summers I escaped from Texas, and once in the Notre Dame library I read the twelfth-century bestiaries and made notes, later lost in a Southern Railway boxcar. In the thirties I jumped freights and thumbed and left my wives (there were three in all) to go discuss me with their mothers.

The third wife, Grace, sat with me in the Houston Hospital while I died. She didn't shed a tear. Grace came late in my life; she never expected much, so was never disappointed. When I loaded up the car, she'd stand in the yard with her arms folded and just say, "Okay, Sunnybitch, don't leave me no dirty laundry." Grace had Indian blood. I miss her calm ways and her slow talking in an alto voice. I've seen her make a face at a coming tornado and then go inside and forget about it. Nothing affected her much. Even sex. She was a challenge. If Grace had cried—even once—in that sterile hospital room, I might have stuck out a finger; I might have blotted that tear and sucked it off and gotten well, just from the novelty of the thing.

She didn't cry, though, and I had not died off into a medieval abbey or a Cherokee camp. You'd think there'd be some choice. They even claim to give you that in the army.

Outside the hut I sat with my book and pen by the lake in the warm sun, reminding myself how the deer had stood and blown the water. Yes, it felt like September here. Indian summer. And for all I knew some real Indian, even a Cherokee with strings of hickory bark around his waist, might step out of these woods. Wonderful!

Might shoot me with his locust bow strung with bear entrails. Not so good. Could I die twice? Re-die? All that was . . . metaphysics. I would not think about it yet.

Could not. The landscape would not allow me. Virginia was opposed to thinking. While I sat in the brightness, empty as a sack, a praying mantis climbed up a weed stalk and lay along its blade. I bent my face beside that green swaying. Red knobby eyes. The only insect, I'm told, that can look over its shoulder. Maybe when this one died of winter, she would be raised up to my scale; as maybe I—shrunken—was now living on the tip of some weed and my lake was a dewdrop in the morning sun.

Yet none of this interested me. The four spread legs, two bent prayer claws, wings folded in layers on her back—I could have watched these tiny things all day, as I had waited for a blue flick on a burning log the night before.

Once I would have touched the mantis to see where she would spring. It was not necessary. I had been let out of thinking as if thinking were a jail. Nothing expected me to connect it with anything else. Not to anticipate—delicious. I felt that first morning the way the baby feels. *I am here.* Nothing else.

Some days went by. My ledger notes are sketchy. Like Thoreau, I gave time to birds and anthills. One afternoon—feeling so far from my other world that I mistook distance for wisdom—I analyzed completely how Western culture fell apart after World War II, and wrote down how this might have been prevented. My words lacked urgency. Nobody would read them. I bored myself.

After burning that, I tried to put on canvas my nighttime deer bent over a floating picture of himself in the black water. My painting was squat and clumsy, a hog at a wallow.

The fifth morning I was sitting on a log by the lake, watching the mist rise. Every morning it lay over the lake like cloud, then slowly churned to blow up the shore and fade among the tree trunks. I watched it begin to thin itself over the land. Down the lake, the mist suddenly shook like a curtain and I had a glimpse of someone walking by the water's edge.

I ran forward a few steps. Like gauze, the air blew shut. I saw it again. If not a man, a bear, upright and moving toward me.

My eye fixed on the fog, I walked in that direction. Fear? I could not remember how it felt to be afraid. In the thinning haze I saw again a—a polar bear? Impossible. White but too small. We could hear each other now. Crackling brush, dry stems breaking underfoot. I moved faster but those other noises stayed unhurried and regular. The mist was waist-high. I walked beyond it into a field of broom sedge and she, at the same moment, worked out of a wispy alder thicket and stared at me. She had on a white uniform, like a nurse.

I called, "Hello!"

She kept one bent alder limb taut in her hand. She was in her late twenties, red-haired, and pregnant. I saw that not only in her shape but the way she stood, bare feet spread wide, her spine tilted. She stepped forward and the branch twanged behind her. "Who are you?"

"My name is Benson Watts. I live . . ." That verb wasn't right. I jerked a thumb over one shoulder. "I've been staying in a little house by the lake."

"Good," she said. "I've not had anything to eat but persimmons. My mouth has shrunk down to zero." She gave me a normal-sized smile as she passed. "This way?"

"Just follow my track. What are you doing here?"

"Eating persimmons is all so far." Flatfooted, she walked along the swath I had made in the ripe weeds. I could not think of a way to ask a pregnant woman if she were dead. I thought about it, but the question sounded impolite. I followed. She was no more than five feet tall. Her short hair was full of beggar's-lice and sticktights.

I said, "Have you been here long?"

"Don't remember."

Her white skirt was streaked with mud and resin. "What's the last thing you do remember?"

"Spending the night in the woods. Oh. There it is." She made for my cabin in that stride which, from behind, looked bowlegged and clumsy. "What's the last thing you remember?"

I decided to say, "A hospital room."

"You're not contagious, are you? TB or anything?" She looked back and I saw how thickly her face was freckled. "You can see why I've got to ask." She patted her belly with her left hand on which she wasn't wearing a single ring. There was a bracelet, though, like mine. I pulled at her tag and turned it over. *Dwell, then travel. Join forces. Disremember.*

"Where'd you get this?"

"The fairies brought it," she said. "And the baby, too." She led the way into my house, stroked the earth floor with the sole of her foot. "This is nice." The tops of her feet were scratched, some of the marks white, some bloodied. I pointed to the pantry. Quickly she ran up to a dangling ham and laid her face on its salty mold. I said I'd slice and fry some. She poked among the pears until she found one mellow enough to eat.

While I chopped off some meat and set the pan in the fireplace, she finished the pear and bit into a cucumber, peeling and all. "What's in this sack?" she called. I was trying to keep the ham from catching fire. "Peanuts!" She crowed, "Oh, glory! Peanuts!" I heard them rattle in a pot. "Let's parch some." She pushed the pan onto a bed of coals and a little grease popped into it and speckled their hulls. "Smell that ham, honey!" she said—not to me, but to the lump at her middle.

I sat back on the dirt floor and let her tend the skillet. "What's your name?"

"Olena."

I had her spell it. I'd never heard that name before. I think she made it up.

"There's flour but no bread," I said. She didn't offer to make biscuits but sat back with her legs crossed wide under the round bulk of her unborn child. I thought through several questions before I chose, "Is your home around here?"

Olena said, "It never was before. Where's yours?"

"Texas." She plucked the fork from my hand and turned over the ham. I took a long breath and blew out a statement on it, watching her. "I was sick in a hospital and then I woke up here."

Olena said matter-of-factly, "I fell down a flight of stairs and this place was at the bottom."

We stared at each other, then quickly looked away. Each of us stole a glance at the pale tag strung to the other's wrist. With a grunt, Olena got to her feet and went to the pantry to find a plate and cutlery. I warned her pork needed to cook longer than that, but she was already spearing an oily slice. "I don't think you can get worms here," she said, staring at the ham.

"I see plenty of regular insects."

Chewing, she didn't care. "Oh, glory, that's good!" she said, with a sigh. I brought her a salt shaker and a tomato with the top cut off; she buried half her freckled face until its juice ran down her chin. "Can I sleep here tonight?" she asked, swiping a forearm over her mouth. I said she could.

Watching her chew the ham and pull its pink shreds from between her teeth, I tried to decide what accident had sent us both here, what kink in orderly process, whether there was some link between our lives or some similarity in our natures which made us candidates for transport to this place. I asked about the location of the stairs where she fell, and Olena said,

"Florida. Fort Lauderdale." All I got out of that was a vague sense of regional districts, but it made me walk to the door and search the edges of the lake for some other Southerner. The mist had cleared.

"What you looking for?"

"Just looking." Somebody else would be coming soon. I felt certain of it. "Olena, is there someplace you're supposed to be? Or be going?"

She finished the ham and raked a pile of peanuts onto the floor to cool. "I guess not."

"We'll wait here for a few days, then."

3

The fire kept me awake. Even with my eyes closed, its pattern of light and shadow on my face was a physical touch and moved like warm water across my skin. I rolled in my blanket farther and farther across the floor and turned my back to the blaze. Above me, in the bunk, Olena lay, spread-legged, bulging. The covers seemed draped on an overturned chair. Behind me, the fire crackled. Rain had begun in late afternoon, so we kept the fire going against a wet chill rising through the dirt floor. Olena's snore was soft as a cat's purr.

I dozed, then leaped alert. What had wakened me? Perhaps that deer, passing my door, had ground his teeth? I threw back the blanket and sat up, listening. It must have been nearly dawn, since mockingbirds were taking turns, each song intensely sweet and swelling higher than the last. Barefoot, I crossed the damp floor and stepped onto the path. Raindrops on the weeds looked solid, like tacks or metal pellets, but the sky was full of fading stars. Far down the lake, something large and dark bent in the mist to drink, too wide and bulky to be a stag. My naked scalp prickled, for there had flared through my head the leaves of those old Latin bestiaries, page after page of winged quadrupeds and dromedaries, each fact of natural history bent to reflect an attribute of Christ. Just from Olena's presence, this landscape had become a dream we both were having and, like those books, took on some quality of concealment and mystery.

I started through the wet grasses to surprise the drinking animal, but it melted through the brush and downhill into the woods, looking odd and fictional. The woods were, at the same time, dark and translucent. It seemed to me even the tree trunks were spelling words I could nearly read. I rested my hand on the bark of one, and tried in its cracks and lichen crusts to make out the Braille. Not since I was a child had I felt this expectancy, as if at last I were on the verge of seeing everything unveiled. Most of my life I'd been certain there was nothing *to* unveil. A bit of lichen, like tough lace, came loose in my fingers.

Quietly, I walked inside the hut, dried my feet, and slid again into my blanket roll. Olena had turned her face to the wall and her back took on a woman's curves. I was fearful of desiring her. I slept and dreamed that my mother was lying on her deathbed and the doctor took a large white bird out of his satchel and wrapped its claws on the brass bedstead. "If the bird turns to face her," he said, "this is not a mortal illness, but if he keeps his back turned there'll be nothing I can do." The bird unfolded extra wings and feathers after being cramped in the leather bag and seemed to grow larger and larger. One at a time, he uncurled his feet and shook them, then flapped once around the room. Each wingbeat sounded like an oar slammed flat against the water. At last the bird lit facing away from my mother, who gave a great cry. I ran forward to beat at the big bird but I could not make it move or even look at me, and its yellow talons were wrapped on the metal rail as if molded there.

At daylight, we were wakened by loud thumps on the wooden door. Olena sprang half out of bed, one of her feet touching the floor.

"Don't worry," I said. "It's another one."

She whispered. "Another what?"

"Another one of us." I jangled my bracelet in the air between us and stepped into my shoes. I dragged open the heavy door.

He was ugly. Malformed—not deformed but *malformed*—six feet tall and the parts of his body mismatched. Hips like a woman and a head flattened on both sides. I could not see a bracelet under the black sleeve of his suit. I pictured him yanked from his mother's womb, not by forceps, but with a pair of cymbals clapped over both ears. His face, driven together by the blow, was long and its features crowded. The nose, buckteeth, popeyes had all pushed forward when the doctor first compressed his skull. "Come in?" he asked softly.

"Of course." Another Southerner—Georgia Cracker by his drawl. "Are you hungry?"

Thinking about it, he rubbed his temples with both thumbs. "I think I just ate," he finally said, and spotted Olena waiting by the bed. "Good morning, Ma'am."

I introduced Olena and myself. He wasn't curious. "Melvin Drum," he said, and wrapped my hand in a long set of fingers. He was too thin for his black suit and the pale bow tie made his Adam's apple look red and malignant. He said politely, "Hate to wake you up."

"We've been expecting you." That puzzled him. He took a seat and stared at his knuckles while he popped each one.

"This is a funny thing," he said mildly. "It might be amnesia. But look here." He leaned his head forward and his longish tan hair divided into two hanks. "You see a knot there? Anything?"

I felt his scalp. "Nothing."

He leaned back and his eyes—which I had thought were blue—glowed green as a cat's. "Maybe I've gone crazy," he said, obviously pleased. "They say religious people do."

Dryly I said I thought Mr. Drum would find he had passed beyond all need for religion now.

He did not hear me. "It's hard to tell nuts from saints," he explained to Olena, "except for God, of course. He can divide them up left and right in the twinkling of an eye. The twinkling. Of one eye." Smiling, he tilted his chair onto two back legs and I grabbed for his sleeve where something gleamed.

"Can you explain this?" I said, shaking my own tag.

"I can accept it," he said. He pulled his cuff over the third bracelet. "We've all passed on and these are our instructions."

"Passed *on*?" said Olena. She crossed to the pantry, carried back a skirtful of yellow apples, and sat on the floor to share them. "Are you certain you're dead, then, Mr. Drum?"

"That was the last promise I heard." His rabbit teeth bit out a sharp triangle and he talked over the sloshing noise of apple in his mouth. "I turned down an alley—there were three men bent over somebody. I tried to run. They grabbed me; one of them put a flashlight on my face and said, 'Oh, Lord, it was Willy and Willy had a big mouth.' The one I couldn't see said, 'Willy's a dead man, then.'"

"Who's Willy?" I asked.

"God only knows." He read the carving softly: "'To avoid

going back—dwell, then travel. Join forces. Disremember.'
Anybody want to go back?"

I pictured myself hooked up to tubes, pumps, catheters,
filling and emptying at the nurses' convenience. No.

But Olena had pressed two freckled hands on her abdomen
and was staring at them while her eyes filled. She sounded
hoarse. "How did you die, then, Mr. Drum? After that
promise?"

Tire iron, lead pipe, he wasn't sure.

"But you were cured of your final . . . condition. Your head
wound. And you, Mr. Watts, of yours. Does that mean? Do
you think I?"

We tried not to look at what her hands were cupping.
Melvin Drum leaned forward and his face shifted in some
way I could not see; his tone dropped down an octave and he
got older and almost dignified as he laid his thin hand on
Olena's red hair. "Sister," he said, nearly rumbling, "leave it to
God."

Water ran down her nose and hung there. "This baby's
alive," she burst out. "You hear me? When the time comes,
you'll have to help me birth. I won't leave that to God." She
shook her head loose from under his hand.

"Yes, you will," he said, but I told her we'd both help and
maybe by then we'd find a doctor, too.

Melvin Drum tapped his bracelet. "We've joined forces,
then," he said. "When does the travel start?"

Tomorrow, we decided. We'd pack food and bottle water.
Olena would rest today and we'd swim, clean our clothes. I
wrote these things down in my green-bound book. "Which
direction shall we take?"

Melvin said east seemed appropriate. I wrote that down.

In the afternoon, he and I floated on our backs in the lake

while Olena hung our clothes on the sunlit bushes. My younger body was a joy to me, moving easily, stroking well. Melvin had a large genital and as we drifted I could sometimes see it shift in the water like a pale fish. "Were you married, Melvin?"

He said no. I thought he must be over thirty. "Were you queer?"

Laughing, he had to gargle out some water. "Very," he said. I don't think he meant for boys.

4

"I'm already tired," Olena complained. "Why must you walk so fast?" On her short legs, she had to make three steps for every one of Melvin Drum's. I was winded, too, and the sun stood directly overhead. "Why hurry?" she puffed, pushing swags of honeysuckle to one side, "when we have no destination and no deadline?"

"None that we *know* of," said Drum, leading the way like the major of a band.

Over her shoulder to me, Olena said, "This is silly. There's no time in this place." Overhearing, Drum pointed straight up at the blazing sun and kept marching. She poked him in the spine above the belt. "Disremember," she said.

We walked noisily, single file, through woods which were thick and shady, their fallen leaves ankle-deep; and the sun slid with us, shooting a ray through a thin branch now and then.

Olena carried the lightest pack—raisins, dried beans, and figs, the peanuts she brought over our objections. Drum and I had mostly ham and wine and water jars. The kitchen knife I'd strung at my waist had pricked me half a dozen times climbing uphill from the lake. The land was level forest now, with no sign of paths or trails.

We rested by a shallow spring with a frog in it. I asked Drum, "You hear a river?" He said it might be. Olena stuck her red hair backward into the spring, so the ends uncurled and hung wetly down her back and dripped on the leaves in front of me when we walked on again.

"I'm ready to unstrap this blanket and leave it on some tree."

Drum told her for the third time we'd need blankets later.

"He thinks we'll still be hiking in December," she grumbled. "He's got a new thing coming." She passed me a pocketful of peanuts to crack and eat as we walked. She wouldn't give Drum any.

The river still sounded far away when we saw it flowing low between walls of thicket and vines which had briers under their heart-shaped leaves. Drum stopped, and we stepped to either side of him and looked downhill. The water was brown and sluggish, with small sandbars in the middle. "Want to camp here?"

"Won't there be snakes?" But Olena let us lead the way and reach our hands back for her when the slope grew slippery or jagged. Rows of black willows kept us from the water's edge, but upstream Melvin Drum broke through to a slab of gray rock which jutted into the current and had built behind it a sandy pool. Olena unlaced my borrowed shoes and slid her feet into it. "Glory, that's cool!" she said and slipped forward until her white hem turned gray in the water.

"It's a good place to build a fire," Drum said, "but we might want to sleep on higher ground."

"I'm so tired all I'd ask a water moccasin is not to snore," she said, lying back and letting her toes float into sight.

Melvin and I dropped our packs to gather firewood and haul it to the rock. I nudged Olena's shoulder once with my toe. "All right?"

"Sleepy," she said. I climbed uphill for another load, thinking that was Drum who thrashed ahead of me through the bushes in the gathering dusk. I squatted to rip lightwood from a rotted stump. Suddenly, from behind, he spoke my name and I jumped up, pointing uphill at the moving underbrush. We watched the dark leaves stir.

"There?" said Drum softly. I saw only a dim trunk of a thick shrub; then it moved and grew a snout. I could make out between twigs the animal's long outline, lean and low to the ground, with a tail curved around its hindquarters. He whispered, "Dog?"

"Wolf," I said. Lupus. Very still, like a carving or a piece of statuary. In slow motion the wolf began to back away uphill, and at one point I could see the whole arch of his back and the curve of his tucked-in tail. Once he stepped on a twig which snapped, and he punished his own paw with a nip. I saw the sharp flesh of teeth. He turned then, and went up the slope in three long bounds.

Drum's breath blew out on the back of my neck. "A real wolf? Here?"

I didn't think it was a real wolf. More like an animated artwork I had seen drawn somewhere, and I said so. "Didn't you see how the shape was exaggerated? It looked so . . . so stylized."

Drum sniffed at his armpit. "Well, I'm real enough. I'm organic and I stink and there's a blister on my foot."

I wanted to tell him about a pictured Lupus who could only copulate twelve days in the whole year and whose female could not whelp except in May and then when it thundered; but that was like saying a twelfth-century picture book had come alive before our eyes, and the Psalter or Apocalypse might be next. For all I knew, Melvin Drum had dream beasts in his own head to which I had yet to be subjected.

We carried down the remaining firewood, pulled the small bag of white beans out of its river soak, and boiled them slowly with a chunk of ham fat in our only pot. While they were cooking, I asked Melvin just how religious he had been.

"The last five years I thought of nothing else." He stretched out on the rock. "It's a shame I'm dead," he said, "because someday I would have finished the stealing and had it all."

"Stealing what?" asked Olena, stirring a peeled stick through the beans.

"Religion. I went in every church I could. Catechisms, hymnals, prayer books, rosaries, creeds—I stole them all. Went on field trips to the Mormons and Christian Scientists. I stacked all that stuff in my room. You could hardly walk for candles and books and shawls." Olena speared a bean for him but he shook his head that it was too hard to eat. "I was in Los Angeles at the end," he said. "On the way to visit the Rosicrucians."

She snapped, "What on earth was it for?"

He smiled at the rising moon. "You ever seen a big set of railroad scales? Where you keep adding weights till the arm is perfectly balanced? When I got all the stuff together, when I had collected the right balance . . . weight . . ." Suddenly he giggled toward the darkening sky. "It sounds dumber now than it did then."

I leaned toward him on both my gritty palms. "Doesn't your head hurt when you remember things like that?"

"No. Does yours?"

Olena said hers hurt, too, just behind both eyebrows. She

spoke in a fast singsong: "So I've quit remembering I was a beautician and having a baby and he was already married and I didn't care and one day I fell down the steps of my apartment building all the way to the washing machines in the basement and the woman folding towels just stood there and hollered all the time I came rolling down and all I could see looking up was her open mouth and fillings in every tooth in her head." She grabbed her forehead. "Whew! That's the last time, damn it." She turned away and for a while the three of us lay flat on our backs on the hard rock, not saying anything, while the sky got darker behind the stars.

The beans took a long time to soften. We got our spoons out of our pockets and tried them and lay down again.

I was almost asleep when Drum said, "Why don't we use the river?"

"Use it for what? To travel, you mean?"

"Beats walking," Olena said.

"If we knew anything about boats or canoes," said Drum.

I sat up. "It happens I know a little." I told them how the Indians would burn down a big tree or find one struck low by a storm, and put pine resin and tree gum on one side and set fire to that, chopping out the charred wood and repeating the blazing gum, until they had burned the log hollow. "Some of their dugouts would carry twenty men."

"Won't that take a long time?" One of Olena's hands climbed up by itself and rubbed her belly.

"We have a rock, water, matches, trees . . ."

Olena pointed her finger at me. "Hah! Why didn't your head hurt? Talking about the Indians, why didn't your head hurt then?"

"I think," said Drum thoughtfully, "it must not hurt if the things you recall are useful to you. Useful now, I mean."

Which, in view of his vague religion, made us stare at him. It was late when we spooned our mushy beans in the dark and rolled up in our blankets, tired enough to sleep on solid stone. If snakes crawled up at night, we never noticed. The last thing I thought was that any serpent I saw in this place would be like the one Pepys claimed could feed on larks by spitting its poison into the air, and for that one I would send forth a weasel, since—as the monks wrote in their illuminated manuscripts—God never makes anything without a remedy.

For all I knew, somewhere in Melvin Drum's last rented room there were stacks of medieval books full of viper-worms and amphisbaenae, and perhaps even stories of the Cherokee Thunders, who lived up in Galunlati, close to that great Apportioner, the Sun.

And Drum was right—thinking of all these things, my head never hurt at all.

5

After that come repeated entries in my ledger: "Worked on boat today."

I don't know how long it took. We had one hatchet and we used sharp rocks. My knuckles bled, made scabs, and bled again.

I slipped into a way of life I seemed to know from the bone out. Squatted in the woods, wiped with a leaf, covered my shit. I peed on tree trunks like a hound—it's instinct, I think. We're meant to give back our excrement to plants. We washed in the river. Even Olena, after a while, bathed with us and I stopped staring at her stretched white skin and the brown mat of hair below. My beard grew out itchy; there were welts across my chest and the beans made gas growl inside us all. One night I spotted the wolf's eyes shining near the rock and I called to him, but the lights stayed where they were. When the ham got moldier, we lived off fish. My finger-nails smelled like fertilizer.

Olena kept saying the boat was done, but I wanted the shell thinner, lighter, and we chopped through the heartwood and sanded the inside down with stones. We pointed the stern and rounded the bow. Even after dark, we'd sit scrub-bing her surface absently with rocks until she felt smoother than our calloused hands.

"She's ready," Melvin Drum said at last. "Admit it, Ben. We can go on."

I did not want to stop. It seemed to me there was grace in the log we had not yet freed, shape that was still unrefined. But finally I gave in. I crushed pokeberries in my palm and wrote on her side with a finger, "*Escarius.*"

They made me explain. A labrus fish, thick-lipped, called by Sylvester "Golden-Eye." The monks had thought the Scar clever, since, when it was trapped in a fish pot—they wrote—it would not dash forward but would turn around and undo the gate with frequent blows of its tail and escape backward. Other Scars, if they saw him struggle, were said to seize their brother's tail with their teeth and help him back loose to free-dom.

We loaded *Escarius,* even filling our water bottles, though we would be afloat in water. We still had beans and damp peanuts, and we opened a jar of grape wine on the rock and poured some on the boat and each spat a swallow into the river—I don't remember why.

Pushing off from the gray rock, we started down the river, Drum and I trying our new poles and paddles. Olena sat amidships and let her fingers trail. She was singing. "Shall we gather at the river? The beautiful, the beautiful river? Gather with the Saints at the river that flows by the throne of God?"

Into the current we moved and skirted the sandbars, slipped silently past the drooping willows, and began an easy drift. The knobs of turtle heads dropped below the water as we drifted by, and floated up again when we had passed. We may have looked majestic, moving downstream in a boat so much longer than we needed. *Escarius* tended to wallow to this side and that, but we learned how to balance with our oars. Our rock went out of sight and the water seemed thick and reluctant and bore us without interest, slowly, while the river spread wider and showed us floodplains and sycamores with watching squirrels.

I felt like a man on a color calendar, poised with my oar level, going off the page and out of sight.

"She's all right," called Melvin Drum. "She rides fine."

Sometimes a snake would drop limp off a low limb and lie on the water like a black ribbon. Olena stopped worrying, since they seemed to fear us and would at the last glide toward the shallow edge and blend with tree roots there. "We're dreaming," she said, turning her face to me. "Even the snakes are dreaming."

The first set of rapids was shallow and we bumped down it like a sledge. Late in the afternoon we pulled up to a low bank under pines and slid the hull over brown needles and braced her ashore with stones. Olena found a tick on her ankle but said it was still a fair place to sleep. My shoulders ached. I walked up the small creek to relieve myself, and on its far side saw the bent tail and stiff fur of the same gray wolf as he slunk away. He could not be the same wolf, yet I was sure he was.

With darkness, the air turned cool and rain spattered overhead. We huddled together under our three blankets but slowly the wool soaked through. Then we just pressed together to outlast the rain, Olena with her back against a pine trunk, Drum and I on either side. Her knees were up, her face down. "I hate it here," she suddenly said. We leaned closer. "I hate it." Putting an arm about her shoulders, Drum and I got tangled with each other, and once I slapped at the wet shreds of his sleeve. "I could have been married by now," she said between her knees. "And had regular customers on my sun porch and bought myself a dishwashing machine." Rain poured over us. "I could have joined the Eastern Star," she wailed.

Trying to rub our foreheads on her soaked hair, Drum and I bumped skulls, and he said angrily, "You let me do all the work today!" Which wasn't so.

When at last the rain stopped, what could we do? We went on sitting there while the moon started down. We were soggy and chilled and had wet wool in our lungs.

In the morning nobody spoke. We spread our clothes to dry and tried to nap but the bugs were too bad.

"We might as well go on," I finally said. I felt resigned. There was nothing at the end of this river but a sea waiting to drown us. It would pull us home like caught fish on a line.

In silence, Drum wadded our wet blankets into the boat. Olena waded out and hoisted herself aboard, and without a word we pushed loose into the current. I was lonely and the river seemed hypnotic, just fast enough not to need our thrust. For a long time we sat with our oars laid in our laps. If Drum watched one bank, I stared at the other, and when his attention shifted I crossed mine over, too.

Once Olena said we should capture the next snake, lift him into the boat, just to see what would happen. Maybe, she said, if one of us was bitten he would move on another layer to someplace else. "We might wake up in the pyramids."

Or Bethlehem, she hoped. I stroked the water hard. Drum grabbed at blackberries hanging from the bank until his hands were purple. I said, "Am I using my paddle enough today? Are you satisfied?"

He said, "It was raining, Ben." We drifted on.

By night we had passed into drier land and could build a fire and string our clothes nearby. We heated a cup of wine apiece. I asked him, "Is there a God? Now? What do you think now?"

"It's hard to think here."

"You can remember, though, better than we can."

The tin cup covered half his face. "I'm like every other expert," he said. "In time, I got interested in the smaller sects. I specialized. Osiris or the voodoo drums. I went to the Hutterites and Shakers. Once I met Frank Buchman and I couldn't see anything special about him. A man had the Psychiana lessons, all twenty-four. It had cost him twenty-six dollars during the Depression; I won't tell you the price he wanted. I didn't pay, of course. I stole the set and hid it in my mattress." He finished the wine. "If a snake bit me, I'd wake up in Moscow, Idaho, asking about Frank Robinson." He said to Olena, "I'd just as soon be here. You feeling better?"

She had fallen asleep, mouth open, the edge of her teeth in view. I knew that I wanted to put my tongue there. I jumped when Drum said, "One thing we mustn't do is fight."

Swallowing, I nodded. He rinsed his cup in the river, stared across its lighted surface. "My brother used to have dizzy fits and he said he dreamed like this. Always of journeys and trips. Mostly he rode on a train that went very fast and roared. He was always on top of the engine, holding to the bells, and the whistle would go right through him, he said. If a tunnel could feel a train go through it, he said he could feel the sound of that whistle, boring, passing." Away from the fire, Drum looked taller. "The dream was always dark except for the engine lamps."

"Where did he go?"

"He woke up too soon."

"Is your brother dead now?"

Melvin Drum laughed coming back into the firelight. He couldn't stop laughing. Even after we had curled up in the damp blankets, I heard him laughing in the dark.

6

How was it possible to dream in that place? Yet I went on dreaming, every night, inventing an overlap of worlds which spun out from me without end. I dreamed of a life in an Indian village ringed by sharpened stakes, where my job was to be watchman over the fields of corn and pumpkins and to run forth with screams and rattles to drive off crows or animals. I dreamed of being alone on a sandy plain, lost, staying alive by eating fly larvae scraped from the surface of alkaline pools.

Drum said he never dreamed. Olena did; she tossed and grunted in her sleep but claimed she could not remember why in the morning.

We blundered on down the river, shipping water, overturning once in white froth when *Escarius* scraped a jagged rock.

"If we took turns sleeping, we could travel at night, too," Drum said; but what was the point now that time did not rush from left to right? Only the river moved—for all we knew, moved forever.

Finally the banks began to withdraw and the wider current slowed. We seldom had to use oars or poles. Early one morning, the shores were suddenly flung outward and we were afloat in a wrinkled lake which seemed without end. Drum said it might be an ocean sound at low tide, since the waves were light but regular. We turned south to keep a shore in view. Soon Drum thrust down with our longest poplar pole and struck no bottom. It flew under the water like a spear and bobbed up far away, beating slowly and steadily toward the sandy bank. Under the hot sun my brain cooked like stew in a pot.

Olena had been silent for a long time. Suddenly she burst out, "You two might be dead but I'm not." Perhaps the child had moved in her, or she imagined that it moved.

Over her head, Drum said to me, "Shall we keep on?" For the first time, he sounded tired.

"Olena?"

She jerked her face away from the disappointing shoreline, so plainly empty of other people like ourselves. Her freckles were wet and her sweaty forehead flamed. "There's nothing here," she said, almost whining. We stroked the water. "You, Melvin Drum, you made us leave that house too soon. Somebody else might have come if we had just waited awhile."

Or, by now, why hadn't we caught up with whoever had burned his books in that fireplace? Yet, I thought, Old Lobo might be the fourth one in our group, and I eyed the shore as if I might spot his gray head sliding through the water, parallel.

The sun had started down the sky when we landed on a small and wooded island pocked with crab tunnels. Drum built a fire and dropped a dozen crabs into boiling water. We carried them in cloths, like hot spiders, up the beach and into the shade of high bushes.

"I'll fix yours," Drum said, breaking off claws, throwing the flippers downhill on the sand. He separated back from body, then gouged down to a paper-thin shell. "Hand me your knife, Ben." He scraped out white meat for Olena and offered it in his palm. She ate bits with her fingers. I cleaned my own. In case there should be some later use for them, we scrubbed the pink shells with sand and set them to dry in the sun. Then, while Olena lay resting under a tree, Drum and I explored the narrow island. There were so many loud birds inland that every tree seemed to scream. We found one pool of brackish water and wild grapevines which still had late fruit, although some had fermented on the stem. We could barely see the shore from which our river had issued, but on the island's far side there was only water and some shadows which might be other islands.

Before dark, the waves grew higher and crabs at their foaming edges carried off the claws and flippers we had thrown. Olena felt pain during the night. Her heavy breathing woke us. She sprang up and began walking on the damp sand, hunched over.

"She's aborting," Drum said, watching her pace.

Olena heard him and screamed that she was not.

"It isn't her time. She's not big enough for that," he added.

I called to her, "When are you due? What month?" But she would not answer.

Drum asked, "How long have we been here, anyway?" I looked back through these moonlit pages trying to count days, but it was hard to estimate. I kept glancing at Olena. Drum jerked impatiently at my book. "Is it forty-nine days? Is it close to that?" I didn't know. He said something about people in Tibet once thinking it took forty-nine days for the passage between death and further life; then he clapped both hands to his head. I stared, for at last there was some piece of remembering that made Drum's head hurt. Good, I thought. I wanted his jaw-teeth roots to burn like fire.

I left him and crossed the sand to Olena. "I'll stay with you." The moonlight turned her hair black and skin gray and sank her eyes into pits. Together we marched on the cool sand. When the pain eased, we dragged her blanket closer to mine and I would feel the knob of her bent knee low in my back like something growing on my spine.

She had rolled to the other side when I woke at sunrise. I turned also, and fitted myself to her back. She only murmured as my arm dropped over her. Our parts were sweetly matched as if she were sitting in my lap; under the curve of her hips I could feel my stiffening heat. My fingers slid past her collar to her loose breast until they could play on her nipple like tongues.

Drum coughed. Over Olena's red curls I saw him watching my busy hand, staring at the cloth where it was moving. I pulled on her skin till the breast budded, all the while letting him watch. Olena was awake now. The cells in her body came alive and caused my own skin to prickle.

Now I yanked my blanket and threw it over both of us, taking care that Drum could see, and that he knew I saw him see.

Under the blanket, creating bulges for his following eye, I ran my long arm over the swell of Olena's child until my thumb was centered low in her body hair and my fingertips pressed on. She moved to help me. I heard her breath. Her leg slid wide and dropped back over mine until I was touching her at last. The hot grasp was too much for me and my spasm came while she was simply widening and making ready for hers. I kept on until she made noises and threw herself on her back, knees up and shivering. Instantly, so Drum could not see her taut face, she jerked up the blanket and pulled it to her eyebrows.

Drum never moved. I gave him a long look, but he never moved. I fell asleep with my hand on Olena's thigh and she must have slept also.

In the morning Drum was gone, and the boat *Escarius* was gone, and half our possessions were neatly laid out by the dried crab shells on the beach. There was a moving speck near the mouth of the river, but I could not tell for sure if it was man or animal and, when the sun got higher, could not find it at all in the glare.

7

Sweet days! Long, languid, poured out like syrup.

Olena slept in my arms. No sex in the regular way— because of her coming child—so, like curious children ourselves, we played touching games on each other's bodies.

Our clothes were very worn. I made a loin wrapping from my torn shirt; she sawed my pants off with a butcher knife for herself and left her breasts naked to the sun. We might have been Polynesian lovers from another age except for our bracelets, which, without ever discussing it, we did not discard.

Maybe ten days, two weeks went by. The nights were cooling but our afternoons were still part of summer. For many meals we dug clams from an inland mudbank, steamed them in salty water.

"Wouldn't you give anything for butter?" Olena said. She had persuaded herself the sea waters were supplying her baby rich brain food and protein. She would watch me slide a knife along a fish's backbone as if each filet were preordained to become some tender organ inside her unborn child. Maybe, she sometimes said half seriously, we should powder the fish-bones since she had no milk to drink?

In spite of the sweet days and sweeter nights, I began gathering wood, poles, stakes, and lashing them together with strings of our ragged clothes or strips of bark. Olena didn't like the raft.

"Where will we go? Not out to sea, and there's nothing ashore but wilderness." She ran a freckled hand around my waist, spun a fingertip in my navel. "You'll help me when the baby comes, Ben. Things will be fine."

But I could hear, in the night wind, winter draw closer than her child. How cold might it get? Which of the fish would stay and what shelter did we have?

She pounded sea oats into flour, mixed that with water, and baked patties in an oven of stones. They were bitter but we ate them for the sake of the different texture. "Now stop working on the raft and let's go swimming," she said. Sometimes I did.

"Isn't it good," she'd whisper to me in the dark, "not to be planning ahead? Saving money? Paying insurance?"

I held her tightly and watched the perpetual sea. "What do you think happened to Melvin Drum?"

Her whole body shrugged. "Who knows?"

Who-knows tormented me more than What-happened. "Maybe," I said, "Drum's found the place by now."

"What place?"

The place it ended. The sweeter Olena felt and tasted, the

more certain I was that this was an interlude we would both forget. Our stay on the island was timeless, so I felt certain it could not possibly last. I had even begun to feel homesick for endings, arrivals. Finality.

"Ooh," breathed Olena, grabbing my hand, "Ooh, glory, feel that!" I laid my palm under her ribs. "Feel him move!"

I held my own breath in case there should be some faint shifting at last below her tight skin. "I feel it," I lied.

She rubbed my chest with her forehead so her long red hair tickled. "When Eve had a son, do you think she worried about who he would marry? We're married, Ben. In a way."

"In a way," I said, kissing the peak of her ear.

"Really, you'll be the baby's father."

The word was not real to me, not in this place. I tested it over and over in my head. Fatherfatherfather until the sound was mixed meaninglessness and prayer. Fatherfather.

"We should have asked Melvin to marry us."

I said, "He wasn't a preacher."

"Never did think that mattered much."

What *had* mattered, after all? Damn headache.

"Surely I'll not get much bigger," said Olena, stroking herself. I thought she was the same size as the first time I saw her walking though the mist. We were both browner, though. Her legs were hairier; on my face grew a broad beard, still not a hair on my scalp. We cleaned our teeth by wrapping wet sand in wads of cloth, or chewing twigs into brushes. Nails on our toes and fingers were long and tough; my foot sole felt like canvas. Sea bathing had hardened our skin and crusted the smallest scratch into a quick scar. My forearms looked almost tattooed.

Yes, we had changed. But Olena was the same size.

One morning there washed on our beach an assortment of

trash which made me shout for Olena. Empty blue bottles, finger-length. A warped black piece of a nameless book cover . . . the foot of a celluloid doll. She grabbed for that—a toy for the baby, she said. I followed the tidemark of seaweed, stirring it with my toes. Rubber tubing. A piece of comb with the teeth sealed by barnacles. A length of wood which had once been fluted, part of a carved chair or table. Olena traced its design with awe, like some archaeologist.

But I was afraid. While she scanned the horizon for sails or a smokestack, I thought of a rent in the membrane between worlds, perhaps the great suck of a filling vacuum which would sweep Olena down more stairs and drop me under another scalpel. When the wind blew, even lightly, it raised goose bumps under my tan. "I've got to finish the raft," I said firmly. All day I watched, while pretending not to watch, for some vessel to follow its trash ashore. The raft grew wide enough for one person. Olena watched openly for a boat. The raft was wide enough for one person and a half. I worked on it constantly. Olena was bored with the building and bracing of its parts, and no longer sat nearby or carried me cooked fish in crab-shell dishes; but sat at a distance on the beach where the flotsam had washed, crooning to the doll's foot and waiting for something to rear up on the line between sea and sky. Some days she did not cook at all. At sundown I would carry food to her. Often she was sitting in an unnatural, stiff position, and kept her hand poised like an eyeshade longer than she should have been able to keep it there.

One evening she used the doll's foot to mash her fish meat into white gruel, then lapped it up with her tongue. I was disgusted and struck her under one eye. I watched tears spill on her reddening cheekbone.

"I'm sorry, Olena. Forget it. Come sleep now."

She shook her head.

"I want you to put your hands on me."

Her eyes were sliding off my face, across the streak of moonlight on the water.

"I'll put mine on you, then," I wheedled.

No. She shrank away on the darkening sand.

When the raft was done, Olena would not climb on. "We're leaving," I said, "even if it is dark." I held the platform still on the water. She would not come and I threatened to hit her again as I had on that other night.

In the moonlight, then, we walked the raft past the low waves till I hoisted her on board and heaved myself beside. Olena wrapped her body and head in a blanket and sat in the middle, a lump, a cargo bale.

"We can cross most of the water in the cool of the evening," I said. All I could see of her was the roundness of one pale heel showing at the blanket's base. I tried to be cheerful. "We might even see Melvin Drum. I bet he made camp on the shore below the river's mouth, and that's right where we'll land." I paddled with wood, with my hands. The raft was slow and awkward and zigzagged on the black water. "Even if Drum moved on, he may have left some clue behind for us. Some message. Why don't you answer me?"

"I don't feel good," said the lump.

We moved very slowly across the wide bay, as if the thick moonlight were an impediment. The edges of the dark water beat luminous on our island and the landfall.

In a loud voice I said, "I couldn't stand just waiting like that. I couldn't keep doing that."

Olena would not move but rode on my labors like a keg under a tarpaulin.

At first light we landed on the same inland shore from

which we had come, although the river was out of sight. No sign of Drum—no old campfires, no heaped shells or stones. The sand piled quickly into low dunes, stubby grass, underbrush.

"Why don't you sleep now?"

"I still don't feel good." Olena tottered up the beach and lay down in her damp blanket while I dragged the raft high from the water. There were shallow paw prints in the wet sand, some in a circle, as if the animal had paced.

I squatted by Olena. "Are you hurting?"

"No." On her back, she stared beyond me. The last stars looked like flecks of paper stuck on the blueing sky. "I feel funny, though."

"It's from leaving. I'm sorry I forced you, Olena."

"Doesn't matter," she said. "But it's colder on this side of the water."

I asked if she wanted a fire, but she said no. I curled up with my head laid on her thighs and went to sleep.

The sun was high and warm when I woke, feeling sticky. Again, Olena was too rigid, with one arm raised off the sand and her palm spread open to the sky. I felt for her knee and squeezed it. "Move around some." Her skin felt cool and dry.

I sat up, staring. Overnight her pregnancy had collapsed like a balloon which had leaked out its air. Without even thinking, I patted the blankets in case there should be a loose baby lying there. No. Nothing at all—no baby, no stains.

"Olena?" I got a good look at her face. She was—what else to call it?—she was dead, her eyelids halfway down. I kissed her cold mouth, which felt hard as a buckle. Then again I kissed her, frantic, blowing my breath deep and pinching her nostrils shut. I was trying to cry without losing the rhythm of the breath and my body shook. I thought my forced air might inflate Olena anywhere, blow up her abdomen or toes, because I did not understand how anything functioned in this place; but nothing happened except that my heartbeat got louder and throbbed in my head until even the sight of Olena lying there pulsated to my eye.

She was dead. I walked away on the beach. I covered her with the blanket and sat there, holding her uplifted hand. I walked some more. I took off every stitch of her clothes and, sure enough, her stomach was flat now as a young girl's. She looked younger, too, fourteen at most, but her face was tired.

I dressed her body again and tried wrapping her hand around the pink doll's foot but there was no grip.

Finally, because I could not bear to put her into this ground, to bury her in Virginia, I laid her on the raft in the blanket and spread her red hair, and combed it with my fingers dipped in water. The bracelet looked tarnished and there was rust in the links of the chain. I placed on her eyes the prettiest coquinas I could find, and she seemed to be staring at the sun with a gaze part pink, purple, pearly. Then I saw I could not push her out to sea without crying, so I wrote in the ledger book awhile, until I could stand to do that.

8

Now it is dark again, and I think I can bear to push Olena off into the waters and let the current carry her down this coast. There have been noises from the thickets at my back. I think the wolf is there.

In a minute I am going to close up this ledger book and wrap it in a strip of wool I have torn off my blanket and put it under Olena's arm, and then I am going to walk waist-deep into the water and watch them both ride away. Who knows where this sea will end, or where Olena will carry the doll's foot and the book? Maybe somewhere there'll be someone to read the words, or someone who dreams he has read them.